"Once again Penelope Wilcock drew me back into fourteenth-century monastic life with a fine mix of descriptive details and evocative language. The peaceful world of St. Alcuin's Abbey is quickly shattered by a violent tragedy and its aftermath, creating genuine heartache, tension, and spiritual angst. The timeless themes woven throughout the pages of *The Hour Before Dawn* spoke to my heart, in particular William's journey of faith and John's hard-won understanding of the power of the Ascension. Even in the darkest moments of the story, hope tarries in the wings. A wonderful writer, a wonderful read!"

Liz Curtis Higgs, New York Times bestselling author,
Mine Is the Night

"*The Hour Before Dawn* takes Penelope Wilcock's saga of life at St. Alcuin's Abbey to the next level. The emotions are real, vivid, and raw. Gritty realism and heart-wrenching suffering are layered into this story, counterbalanced by redemptive tenderness and noble self-sacrifice. Wilcock weaves a tale of complex interpersonal relationships against the backdrop of a medieval monastery. This novel is a brilliant exploration of what it means to be human—and more importantly, what it means to be a human remade in the image of Christ."

Bryan Litfin, Professor of Theology, Moody Bible Institute;
author, *The Sword, The Gift,* and *Getting to Know the
Church Fathers*

"Penelope Wilcock has created a wonderful cast of characters for her medieval series. *The Hour Before Dawn* deals with the universal theme of evil and the Christian response, and sets the tale in a marvelously accurate fourteenth-century monastery. For the lover of medieval mysteries this is a book not to be missed."

Mel Starr, author, *The Unquiet Bones, A Corpse at St. Andrew's
Chapel, A Trail of Ink,* and *Unhallowed Ground*

"*The Hour Before Dawn* shows vividly how the wrenching horror of cruelty can be overcome by the unspeakable beauty of restoration. I know of no other writer who sees so clearly into the souls of her characters as does Penelope Wilcock. And she sees with such humor and love. Her prose is like rich, dark chocolate poetry. This book offers a deep well of mercy and grace and forgiveness—even forgiveness of self. Drink from it."

Donna Fletcher Crow, author, *Glastonbury: The Novel
of Christian England, A Darkly Hidden Truth,* and
The Monastery Murders

Praise for The Hawk and the Dove Series

"Poignant, moving, rich with imagery and emotion. . . . Modern readers will easily identify with each character in Wilcock's timeless human dramas of people learning to love and serve one another while growing in their understanding of a tender and compassionate God. Highly recommended reading."
Midwest Book Review

"This is a wonderfully insightful series, with a rich historical storyline. There's more substantial content here than in much Christian fiction—about grace, about leadership and loyalty, about humility, about disability and suffering."
FaithfulReader.com

"The series keeps getting better and better. What a delight first-time readers of this series have ahead of them!"
Donna Fletcher Crow, author, *Glastonbury: The Novel of Christian England, A Darkly Hidden Truth,* and *The Monastery Murders*

"This masterful look into a bygone era reminds us that Christians of every age have faced the same basic struggles: how to worship God in spirit and truth and to love our neighbors as ourselves. The inhabitants of St. Alcuin's Abbey reveal a piety that is foreign to many believers today—and is in sore need of recovery. Many thanks to Penelope Wilcock for showing us, through the power of literature, an old way to new life."
Bryan Litfin, Professor of Theology, Moody Bible Institute; author, *The Sword, The Gift,* and *Getting to Know the Church Fathers*

"The stories are truly new, nothing that is cliché or commonplace. The writing is crystalline and beautiful but also simple. . . . I hold this series up with *The Wise Woman* by George MacDonald and *Perelandra* by C. S. Lewis for the lessons it taught me and for the beauty it showed me. It is a truly redemptive story."
P. J. Wong, New Mexico

"Perhaps the most devotional, grace-filled Christian fiction I've read since Francine Rivers's *The Mark of the Lion* trilogy."

Christina Moore, Texas

"This series is warm and beautiful, lighted with an unforgettable ambience. Wilcock highlights the need to understand and embrace those who find themselves marginalized and relegated to loneliness in our church community—the deaf, the mentally handicapped, and the incontinent, to name a few. I highly recommend this series to all who wish to be both entertained and challenged."

Rosemary C. Freeman, Kansas

"We have used Wilcock's books as devotionals at our staff meetings over the years and they have been an amazing tool in discipleship, particularly with people that struggle with self-loathing. But they also are great tools for plain, old-fashioned evangelism, for people who are nowhere near the inquiry road to truth. This series has opened many doors."

Elvira McIntosh, Australia

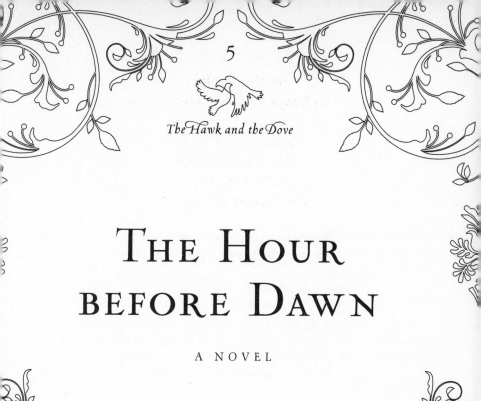

The Hawk and the Dove

THE HOUR BEFORE DAWN

A NOVEL

PENELOPE WILCOCK

CROSSWAY

WHEATON, ILLINOIS

The Hour before Dawn

Copyright © 2012 by Penelope Wilcock

Published by Crossway
     1300 Crescent Street
     Wheaton, Illinois 60187

Cover design: Amy Bristow

Cover illustration: Shannon Associates, Glenn Harrington

First printing 2012

Printed in the United States of America

ISBN-13: 978-1-4335-2659-6
ISBN-10: 1-4335-2659-X
PDF ISBN: 978-1-4335-2660-2
Mobipocket ISBN: 978-1-4335-2661-9
ePub ISBN: 978-1-4335-2662-6

Library of Congress Cataloging-in-Publication Data
Wilcock, Penelope.
    The hour before dawn / Penelope Wilcock.
        p. cm. (The hawk and the dove ; bk. 4)
    ISBN-13: 978-1-4335-2659-6 (tp : alk. paper)
    ISBN-10: 1-4335-2659-X
    1. Monks—Fiction. 2. Monastic and religious life—History—
Middle Ages, 600–1500—Fiction. 3. Historical fiction, English.
4. Christian fiction, English. I. Title.
PR6073.I394H68   2011
823'.914—dc22   2011020701

Crossway is a publishing ministry of Good News Publishers.

BP   21   20   19   18   17   16   15   14   13   12
14   13   12   11   10   9   8   7   6   5   4   3   2   1

FOR
JULIE BALMER and JEHANE HARLEN,

friends far away
who have encouraged and supported me
with humor and kindness,
patience and gentleness,
prayed me through
dark times and difficulties,
walked with me in spirit,
listened to my doubts and fears,
reminded me of my faith
and how well placed it is
in a God who,
no matter how bad things look,
will never give up on us,
never desert us,
and brings us through to
new hope, new life, new possibilities.

THE HOUR BEFORE DAWN

In that last hour before dawn,
when hope still lay hidden by the darkness,
Jesus said to Mary, who had come to the tomb
where his broken body had been left:
"Do not cling to me,
for I have not yet ascended to the Father;
but go instead to my brothers and say to them,
'I am returning to my Father and your Father,
to my God and your God.'"
JOHN 20:17

Open are the gifts of God
Gifts of love to mind and sense
Hidden is love's agony
Love's endeavour, love's expense.
W. H. VANSTONE

He has stumbled on this hole
in the bad hour before the dawn.
WILLIAM BUTLER YEATS

CONTENTS

Acknowledgments and More

*T*he verse of W. H. Vanstone's hymn included with the quotations in the front of this novel is taken from *Love's Endeavour, Love's Expense* by W. H. Vanstone, published and copyright 1977 by Darton, Longman and Todd Ltd., London, and used by permission of the publishers.

Special thanks to Alice and Hebe Wilcock, whose tireless and ingenious researches in the field of medieval monastic and medical detail helped so much and whose intimate familiarity with the life and times of the Benedictines of St. Alcuin's Abbey saved me some unfortunate gaffes.

Special thanks also to Tony Collins, five years my husband, more than twenty years my publisher and trusty editor, who read the manuscript with a seasoned editorial eye and, even more importantly, paid most of my living costs and ironed his own shirts, leaving me free to write the book.

And I am given to understand that Brother Conradus would like to offer his most humble and hearty thanks for the recipe he found in my *Country Living* magazine for sorrel and spinach quiche. He says nettles will do just as well as spinach, but you do have to pick them young—and please use only the tops.

THE COMMUNITY OF
ST. ALCUIN'S ABBEY

(Not all members are mentioned in *The Hour before Dawn*.)

Fully professed monks:

Abbot John Hazell	*formerly the infirmarian*
Father Chad	*prior*
Brother Ambrose	*cellarer*
Fr. Wm. de Bulmer	*cellarer's assistant (formerly an Augustinian prior)*
Father Theodore	*novice master*
Father Gilbert	*precentor*
Brother Clement	*overseer of the scriptorium*
Father Dominic	*guest master*
Brother Thomas	*abbot's esquire, also involved with the farm and building repairs*
Father Francis	*scribe*
Father Bernard	*sacristan*
Brother Martin	*porter*
Brother Thaddeus	*potter*
Brother Michael	*infirmarian*
Brother Damien	*helps in the infirmary*
Brother Cormac	*kitchener*
Brother Richard	*fraterer*
Brother Stephen	*oversees the abbey farm*
Brother Peter	*ostler*
Brother Josephus	*acted as esquire for Father Chad between abbots; now working in the abbey school*
Brother Germanus	*has worked on the farm, occupied in the wood yard and gardens*
Brother Mark	*too old for taxing occupation, but keeps the bees*
Brother Paulinus	*works in the kitchen garden and orchards*
Brother Prudentius	*now old, helps on the farm and in the kitchen garden and orchards*
Brother Fidelis	*now old, oversees the flower gardens*
Father James	*makes and mends robes, occasionally works in the scriptorium*
Brother Walafrid	*herbalist, oversees the brew house*
Brother Giles	*assists Brother Walafrid and works in laundry*

| Brother Basil | *old, assists the sacristan—ringing the bell for the office hours, etc.* |

Fully professed monks now confined to the infirmary through frailty of old age:

Father Gerald	*once sacristan*
Brother Denis	*scribe*
Father Paul	*once precentor*
Brother Edward	*onetime infirmarian, now living in the infirmary but active enough to help there and occasionally attend Chapter and the daytime hours of worship*

Novices:

Brother Benedict	*assists in the infirmary*
Brother Boniface	*helps in the scriptorium*
Brother Cassian	*works in the school*
Brother Cedd	*helps in the scriptorium and when required in the robing room*
Brother Conradus	*assists in the kitchen*
Brother Felix	*helps Father Gilbert*
Brother Placidus	*helps on the farm*
Brother Robert	*assists in the pottery*

Members of the community mentioned in earlier stories and now deceased:

Abbot Gregory of the Resurrection	
Abbot Columba du Fayel (also known as Father Peregrine)	
Father Matthew	*novice master*
Brother Cyprian	*porter*
Father Aelred	*schoolmaster*
Father Lucanus	*novice master before Father Matthew*
Father Anselm	*once robe maker*

CHAPTER
ONE

om!"

Brother Thomas thought he had never heard a monk shout so loud.

He stopped and turned round. He had never seen Brother Martin run before, either. Brother Martin did not have the physique for running, and Brother Thomas watched in fascination. The sight was decidedly comical. He remembered that moment, afterwards, as the last time he found anything funny for a very long time.

"Tom!" Brother Martin was puffing now and bent down to get his breath, his hands on his knees. "Tom, for the sake of all holy, make haste over to Father John's lodging. Go now."

Brother Thomas asked the obvious question: "Why?"

And when Brother Martin told him in puffs and gasps what had happened, "Oh *Jesu Christe!* Oh mother of God!" Tom murmured in horror and shock as he listened, then said nothing further, but turned back toward the cloister, going with all speed to the abbot's house. Outside the door, which was closed, he stood for a moment. He realized that he needed courage to go in. He prayed, silently: *God, help us now . . . help us now. . . .* He lifted the latch but didn't knock.

On a stool that stood randomly in the center of the room, Abbot John, sat as he had sunk down when he heard the news. His face was so white it looked almost green. His hand was pressed against his mouth. He stared without seeing. He responded not at all to Tom's entrance. He was shaking all over. He was alone. Brother Martin, who had run to relay the news to him, he had sent away with a disconcerting impression of complete calm: "Will you leave me, Brother? I think I need to be by myself a little while."

His voice had been quiet, but his tone admitted no question of argument or remonstrance to Brother Martin's mind. As Martin withdrew unobtrusively, leaving his superior in privacy, it came to him that this caliber of being was what made an abbot: the capacity to stand like a rock however mighty the breaker that crashed down. Even so, amid his admiration he had the sense to recollect that Father John was human and bethought him to go in search of his abbot's esquire.

Brother Thomas held in his heart as something precious the privilege of his obedience: even so, there were moments when his inner being quailed before the prospect of walking so intimately close beside a man strong in spirit—and this was one of those moments. But he did not shirk it.

Tom crossed the room to his abbot and waited, feeling the intensity of what was here, his face sober, saying nothing. John turned his head to glance at him momentarily, let his hand drop.

"Don't touch me," he said abruptly. "Please don't touch me. I think I'll just break if you touch me."

And Tom stood looking at him—awkward, horrified, feeling the waves of shock and appalled sorrow for what felt like a lifetime, resisting the temptation to run away.

"I don't see how I will ever be able to take this in," John eventually said. Then, "Could you just leave me alone a bit longer?"

So Tom did. He hesitated, and then he went away.

✠ ✠ ✠

Katelin Hazell was neither a heretic nor a witch. She was not lewd, and she was not a blasphemer. When the priest of her village warned his parishioners, in dark and meaning tones, "When a woman thinks alone, she thinks evil," he spoke ignorantly and made himself the mouthpiece of others.

Katelin's daughter, Madeleine, was no more a witch or heretic than her mother. She was strong in spirit, and she stood straight and spoke straight, it was true, but that should not have told against her. When Madeleine had a point to make, she would look a man in the eyes as well as a woman, and that never weighed in her favor. Her wit was too clever, and rumor had it she knew how to read and her mother had taught her, but nobody ever proved that.

Even while Katelin's man, Jude, still lived, the village saw him little, for he was a soldier, which took him away in the king's service more than it left him in peace with his family at home. As well as her daughter, Katelin had a son, Adam. But he had gone north to the hills to live as a monk on the edge of the moors somewhere, and people talked. Two women together looked like a coven, frankly—especially two women who stood straight and needed no help and talked as cleverly and forthright as men. And 'twas said they could read, both of them, and who had taught them, with no men in the house, if not the very Devil himself? Besides that, why had their men left them like that? Why could they not abide their women's company? Everyone knew that witches could turn men into beasts by their magic acts. Katelin said her man had died in the war; she said her son had gone into a monastery. Who knew but she spoke lie upon lie? And . . . she kept goats. True, they were she-goats for the most part in her flock. But folks had seen her huge sneering billy with the yellow slotted eyes, standing proud on the manure heap and looking down on his harem and spraying into the wind with a great stink. Sometimes the Devil took the form of a goat when he presided at the witches' sabbaths, where they worked great evil with their books and their herbs, their chickens and their wicked plots and their foul knowledge.

And why did she live up on the hill in that cottage alone? If she thought herself too good for the village, that looked bad enough—but maybe it was something far more sinister? Some said they had seen her standing in the moonlight, singing, combing her long silver hair as she stood in that garden. How brazen was that? To let her hair down and comb it, outdoors! Why did she stand there like that in the garden? Whom did she hope to attract? Perhaps it was the Devil goat she sought to lure into her house off the manure heap, for concupiscence, for the satisfying of her filthy, insatiable lusts?

It was true, folks knew it well, that no murder or theft, no adultery or violence could be blamed on Katelin or Madeleine— at least not directly. If they were witches, they were blessing-witches, but they belonged no less to the Devil if they were. They healed with simples, with poultices and tisanes when folk came to them for help, but who was to say they had not polluted the plants and the vials of physic with charms and incanta-tions? What was Katelin singing in the night garden under the crescent of the moon? It sounded like the *Salve Regina*, but maybe it was a foul perversion of the sacred original.

And Madeleine, with her long-tailed, laughing eyes—what was she working, what was she plotting? Those who brought their ulcers and boils and coughs to her she could make well; yet she was no priest, but only a woman! Whose power had she invoked?

When a baby was coming, sometimes the other village women would send for Katelin and Madeleine to help, and they had herbs to help the pain. If a woman carrying a child began her pains too early, sometimes Katelin's herbs and her advice could avert the loss. They knew herbs to help knit broken bones and herbs to soothe skin irritations and herbs to help pains in the gut and bad wind. Either one of the women would look at the urine of a sick man to read its meaning or touch his wrist or his neck to feel his pulses, which the priest never did when someone called him in to pray for the sick. They had about them all the signs of cunning-folk.

When someone died, they would come, the two of them, if they were called upon—but who knew why? Was it merely what it seemed—to wash and to lay out the dead, to comfort folk prostrated with grief, to calm and support and help them through? Or were they most cunning of all in those times, making use of the grief of God-fearing honest families to work their own loathsome schemes, sucking the souls of the dead out of corpses when no one was looking?

Why did they love the stars as well as the wholesome sun? Was it not because the hare is also a magical creature and a worshiper of the moon? Perhaps on her nightly prowl the old woman might take the form of a hare or fly through the air. Perhaps it was she who was to blame when Goodwife Smith's best spotted fowl mysteriously stopped laying and within the week fell dead. Might it have been Madeleine's shadow falling on the milk that curdled it so quickly? When they killed a rooster, was it only for the pot—or were they up to some gruesome practice that would make your flesh crawl if only you knew?

They had been seen—both of them—smelling the fragrance of flowers, their eyes closed and the pleasure of it plain on their faces. They'd been seen standing together listening in rapture to the singing of some blackbird or robin or wren. They never dressed in scarlet—unless their undergarments secretly were—but they wore blue and green dresses of their own dyeing, never gray, and even their brown cloaks were rich russet. Everyone knew how the Devil slips down secret channels of color and music and scent, slips secretly into the soul, like an insect into the ear of a sleeping man. And sometimes they had been seen laughing and laughing and laughing—laughing until they were helpless with laughter and had to hold onto each other. And for what good reason could that possibly be—one of them of an age that her womb was shriveled and dry, the other with no man of her own and never had one?

They came to Mass, it was true, and blessed themselves with holy water when they came into the church. Eyes watched them closely to see if they fell twitching and shrieking or if steam hissed out of their ears as the holiness tormented an occult spirit that lodged like a parasite hooked in their souls, but that had never happened—yet.

The year before Katelin's lad had gone away "to the monastery," an itinerant healer had been that way—an infidel and a foreigner who didn't know the words of the Mass and couldn't rehearse the *Pater Noster*, nor yet the *Ave Maria*—worse than a heretic. And he had lodged with Katelin and spent time in conversation with the boy, brought him alongside him into the homes of the sick, showed him all manner of tricks and wonders. It was after that the lad had gone away; so maybe it was to no monastery after all. Maybe he was a witch himself, for he had learned to read, and certainly he hadn't learned that from Father Aelfric, who knew his letters but sometimes got numbers upside down. But that was many years ago now. In that time the witch's power would have steadily increased. And in those days no one had thought twice about a wisewoman or about women living alone. Now folk had rumbled their rebellion, the unsubmissiveness of their souls.

"Thou shalt not suffer a witch to live," so says the Holy Bible, and His Holiness, God's Vicar in Rome, had only the year before authorized the Inquisition to hunt down sorcerers. The links were starting to be made between village wisewomen and sorcery and heresy. The fires that would rage across Europe for centuries were beginning to be kindled now. It was word of this that fanned the flames of whispering in the village, especially after Elspeth Kempe said she knew for sure that Katelin was a heretic, and if Katelin, then surely Madeleine too. Elspeth swore Katelin had averred that a soul could be saved by Christ alone, without the holy sacrament or the blessing of the priest, but only by simple faith and the love of God in the heart. She said the spirit was free like a bird and belonged to no hierarchy. She said every institution was a construct of man's devising. She said the church could never make a net fine enough to snare the Holy Spirit; it had no monopoly on holiness. Katelin said altogether too much, and she had no doubt poisoned her daughter, Madeleine, with the sulfur of her folly.

And one night when a child had died mysteriously and a man had caught a pox he couldn't account for, it became convenient to find somebody to blame. The wisewomen should be confronted and their wicked arts brought to an end; the devil that stood proud on the manure heap should be gelded.

It was not meant to become the big thing that it did. The men had been drinking and were egged on by the ill will of spiteful women. The man with the pox had a reason to divert the attention of his wife. They took a couple of torches to light the way along the lane, and eight of them climbed the track that led up the hill to Katelin's cottage, filling the night with loud laughter and lewd jests about Katelin's goat and about women who rode on broomsticks.

When they got to the cottage, they went for the goat first, in a drunken, unfocused way, but he made a commotion and knocked them flying, and then someone picked up a stone and threw it at the house, shouting, "Witch! Come out, witch!" Madeleine had been sitting beside the fire with her mother, the two of them dressed in their nightgowns and shawls, combing their hair (one dark head, one silver) and chatting as the wing of night folded them in. She came out to see what was happening when the stone hit her door with a thud, and she called the intruders every name imaginable when she saw who was there. While she stood raging at them someone had the idea of searching the house for books that might speak against the teaching of the church. Katelin, also in the doorway now, protested. A tussle followed, one of the men shoved Katelin so roughly into the house that she lost her balance and fell, and the crowd, all pushing to get in, set fire to the thatch with their torches by accident.

Madeleine took off her shawl to try and smother the flames before they got out of control as three of the men stumbled into the cottage and five of them staggered around her garden, trampling the herbs and catcalling and whooping incoherently. She shouted at them to get off their land and leave them in peace and ran after them as they went for the billy goat again. This time one of them grabbed her and held her fast, while one of the others caught the goat by its horns, and a third made a cruel mess of a bloody castration. They had Madeleine now, and the violence and excitement aroused them. "This what you like, witch?" one of them taunted her, groping at her body as his friend held her fast. The more she struggled and swore at them, the more it inflamed them. One of them ripped her nightgown, laughing, and she spat at him and aimed a kick.

Inside the house three men ransacked the clothes chest and the cupboard, then tore down the bundles of drying herbs from the rafters. Katelin had staggered to her feet and grabbed the sleeve of one of her intruders, but he lashed out at her in fury, knocking her to the floor, where she lay still. Finding a leather bottle of good wine, the men in the cottage passed it round, drinking by turns until it was empty.

Outside, the fire had taken hold in the thatch. "Take a look at this, witch! What d'you think of what's coming to you now, witch?" the men jibed in the garden. They flung Madeleine to the ground and held her down. She fought like a wild animal, but they were too many for her. When she would not lie still, they banged her head on the ground until she did. When they had finished with her, for good measure they cut the goat's throat. The cottage was ablaze by now, and the men who had rummaged through its contents rolled out disappointed to find nothing but the pots and cooking vessels of an ordinary house: no books of spells, no charms or amulets, nothing of significance but the simple wooden cross that hung on the wall. As the lust of power and sex and self-righteousness began to leave them, drunk though they were, the men felt it better to get away from the place. They left Madeleine unconscious and bleeding in the garden by the slaughtered body of the goat. When she came to toward morning, the cottage, still burning, was almost gone, and Katelin was dead. The vegetable garden was trampled and the door to the goat shed banging in the wind. Her little herd was gone.

Dazed and half-naked in the torn, bloody filth of her nightgown, afraid to go into the village for help, afraid to stay where she was in case they came for her again, afraid to be seen in her shame, Madeleine hid in the woods until dusk came again, when she made her way to the house of Poor Clares that had been built down by the river. They took her in, these good women, and asked if she had any family. "Only my brother, Adam," she said, "whose name in religion is John; he is the abbot at St. Alcuin's high up on the edge of the moors."

So the sisters sent word to John. Their Mother Abbess felt a profound sense of sympathy, not only because of the sickening and distressing nature of the tragedy, but because she knew John Hazell had been made abbot no earlier than the middle of Lent. It was now still only two weeks into Eastertide. She prayed for him. There was only so much that could hit one man at once and leave him still standing.

☩　　☩　　☩

Father William stood talking with Brother Michael in the infirmary's small dispensary.

"What sphagnum moss we need, we usually gather ourselves," Michael was saying. "Also each time any of the sheep

25

are slaughtered, Brother Stephen usually keeps back three skins for us. We use them for anyone who can't get out of bed; a sheepskin is the best thing against pressure sores and wondrous comfortable to rest a painful body on. We badly need some more oil; almond is what we generally use, but any will do. Sometimes when we've run out, I've had to use poultry grease, but even with the aromatics in, that still smells foul. We are running low on aromatic oils too, and, as ever, we can do with any linen, however small a piece. We're as careful as we can be, but we still have to throw pads and bandages away sometimes—or burn them if we think there is any contagion. We do our best, Father; truly we are never wasteful, but I think this is going to come up costing very dear, isn't it? We'll be grateful for whatever can be afforded."

William considered the list he had made.

"If you asked for silk sheets and silver chamber pots, the price would be as nothing compared with the compassion and kindness and sheer hard slog there is in this infirmary," he said. "I'll see what I can do—consulting with Brother Ambrose, of course." Though Father William had a complete grasp of every facet of the abbey's domestic economy, he held firmly in mind that he was newly received and merely the cellarer's assistant; he took care to observe the appropriate formalities.

They both looked up in surprise as Brother Thomas, out of breath, appeared in the doorway.

"What's wrong?" asked Michael with one look at Tom's face.

"It's Father John." Tom shook his head and stopped to catch his breath. Alarmed, Brother Michael slid from the tall stool on which he had been sitting by the dispensary workbench, ready to answer the need, but Tom raised a hand to delay him. William stood, silently alert, waiting to hear what he had to say.

"No, it's not like that—phew—just a minute, I came at a run." His brothers waited, and a few seconds later Tom continued. "Sorry—that's better. There came a messenger, just after the midday meal, with news from the monastery of Poor Clares near the village where Father John's family lives. His mother and sister—I don't think you've met them, William, but neither one of them is your run-of-the-mill housewife. They can both read and keep accounts, they're both wise with herbs and healing and midwifery. Anyway it would seem there have been murmurs—these accusations are not true—suggesting witchcraft and heresy. The sisters say his mother has been put to death and his sister violated. Their home was burned and all they had destroyed. Madeleine has taken refuge with the sisters."

"Oh, Jesu mercy!" said Michael. William said nothing at all but stood very, very still, his eyes fixed on Brother Tom.

"Who is with Brother John?" asked Michael next.

"Father John," Tom corrected automatically. "He is alone. That was his wish. I ran straight to him. He sent Martin away when he heard the news. I went to him, but he asked me to go away too."

"Hmm. I understand. God bless him, he probably needs a bit of space. Brother—sorry, *Father*—John is a healer, but he's not . . . well, he needs solitude as much as company. Anyhow, they will be ringing the bell for None shortly, I imagine. Will you go, Tom, and if John doesn't appear in chapel, explain to Father Chad and ask him to stand in? I'll mix him up some physic here to help with the shock, and we can be on hand for when the companionship of others feels more welcome."

While Michael was speaking, William quietly left the room.

He walked rapidly across to the cloister buildings through the bright May sunshine and, when he reached the abbot's house, knocked gently on the door. No reply came from within. William paused, then lifted the latch quite noiselessly and let himself in with no sound at all.

John still sat exactly where Brother Tom had found him and left him, on the stool in the middle of the room. William did not go near but sat down on the floor with his back against the wall next to the door. He did not speak; he barely even breathed; he bent his head and did not look at John. He just waited.

Some fifteen minutes later, the bell for None began to sound, but John did not stir.

In the chapel, amid the whisper of robes and sandals of the community flowing in like a purposeful river of prayer, Brother Tom slipped unobtrusively to Father Chad's side as he came in through the door.

"Father, a word." Tom spoke in an undertone, so he could just be heard but no more. "Father John has had bad news. His mother has died, and his sister has been hurt in an attack on their home. I think he may not come for prayers."

"How long have you known this?" demanded Father Chad. Tom thought he sounded indignant, even in a whisper.

"Hardly any time. The message came this afternoon."

"Why did you not send for me at once?" Father Chad asked, affronted. "I must go to him immediately!"

"No!" Brother Tom laid a detaining hand on his arm. "He wants no one, Father. He asked to be left alone. He sent me away." He looked at Chad beseechingly. "Don't trouble him. Look after the office for him. Please."

Father Chad nodded. "Very well. That seems wise." He glanced around the chapel. By now the brothers were all seated. They knew, as brothers in community always know, even those few whom the word flying around the abbey had still not reached, that something was badly amiss.

"Where's William de Bulmer?" whispered Father Chad suspiciously.

Tom shook his head. "I have no idea. Were they seeing tradesmen this afternoon perhaps?"

"Yes, but Brother Ambrose is here!"

Certainly it was hard to explain the cellarer's assistant's absence if their cellarer was free to come to chapel. Tom could think of no further diplomatic ruses for throwing their prior off the scent. "Oh, well, I just don't know," he mumbled.

Father Chad looked uneasy. "Take your seat, brother," he instructed. "I'll go along and comfort Father John as soon as the office is sung."

He strode purposefully to the abbot's stall as Tom slipped into his. "Will he not see you?" whispered Theodore to Tom.

"No one," he replied under his breath. "He looks just dreadful."

Father Chad gave the invitation, "*Dominus vobiscum*," and the community gathered their various thoughts into common prayer.

Twenty-five minutes later, the afternoon office having ended, footsteps approached the abbot's door, and somebody knocked with determination. William raised his head and looked for his abbot's reaction. John moved as if searching for escape, and the expression on his face told William he could not yet bear the intrusion of human company.

"Go into your chamber," said William, peremptory and very low.

John sighed. He had been aware of William's presence, but he did not look in his direction. The knock at the door came again, and this time whoever stood outside put his hand to the latch. At that, with the swiftness of a hunted animal, John went through to his chamber and shut the door. The sound of this was masked by the rattle of the iron latch lifting and falling on the outer door. When it opened, William was already on his feet, poised to answer. With a movement that looked like casual greeting, he put his right hand on the latch and lifted his left to the door frame, making it impossible to pass.

"Father Chad," he said, "thank goodness you've come!"

"I came as soon as I was alerted to the dreadful news," said the prior. "I don't know why I was not told earlier—did you know before? You must have or you would not be here!"

"I was not told, Father," said William meekly. "I happened to be standing there when the message came and thought to see if I could be of assistance. Brother Martin naturally came to tell Father John first, and of course Brother Thomas as his esquire would be on hand. No doubt Brother Martin was still searching for you when the bell began ringing for None, and he expected to see you in chapel."

Father Chad nodded, somewhat mollified by this version of events.

"I stood in for Father John in chapel," he said confidingly. "I came straight from there to offer my comfort and condolences. Is he not here?"

William bowed slightly in affirmation and to convey a subtle impression of respect and deference. "He retired into his chamber, Father Prior, and will see nobody—nobody at all, not even those closest to him like yourself. The bad news has hit him hard, and he is not yet ready for expressions of goodwill."

"I wonder if I should come in and wait . . . " Father Chad mused. But William stood firm. "My lord prior," he said, "you will of course know better than I what is wisest and best, but may I suggest it could be prudent to verify with the guest house, the kitchen, and Brother Thomas if Father had any hospitality planned for tonight? If he is expecting visitors to eat with him, you might make a change in the arrangements and dine with them yourself in the guest house—so they will still feel they have had the opportunity to meet with a senior brother of real importance. If on inquiry you find he is expecting no visitors, you might come back and see if he is ready to receive you after Vespers? Either way I think he will be relying on you to lead Vespers for him."

"Good plan!" Father Chad seemed pleased with this proposal and the way it had been put to him. "Thank you, Father William, for your good sense. May I ask you to continue at your post here until I or someone else comes to relieve you?"

"I am glad to do as you ask, Father," murmured William submissively. As Father Chad turned away and headed purposefully along the cloister, William closed the door again and sat down on the floor just beside it, as before.

Another half hour passed, and then the door to the inner chamber opened again. John stood in the doorway.

"Thank you," he said tonelessly. "Thank you."

He walked into his room, wandering restlessly from the doorway to the chair by the fire, then to his worktable, then came to rest, just standing. He looked down at the table, tracing his fingertips on its edge.

"What now?" he asked in the same flat voice. "What on earth should I do now?"

"You should make arrangements to visit your sister and bury your mother, my lord," replied William quietly.

John stared at him, dazed. "Make arrangements? I don't think I can organize to put one foot in front of the other." He shook his head, uncertain. He looked bewildered and lost. "This is awful. I've always been incisive, known what to do . . . William—will you help me; if I go there, will you come with me?"

William got to his feet slowly, the time this took giving him a small space to consider the request. He had no wish to antagonize Father Chad by usurping any role he might feel to be his due as St. Alcuin's prior; and even less did he wish to make Brother Thomas, the abbot's esquire, feel in any way slighted. Harder to admit to himself was his fear of leaving the safe boundary of St. Alcuin's walled enclosure. It was too little time since he'd been a hunted man, seeking refuge from the hatred and vengeance of his enemies. He was afraid of being recognized, afraid to face being reviled, afraid to think of the attack on Madeleine and to wonder what rough justice could still threaten him in the world outside the sturdy protection of these walls. All this passed through his mind in a flash as he moved from sitting to standing, feeling profoundly ashamed of himself that when it came to it and John actually asked him to do something in return for all his kindness, William thought he was probably going to say no. He wished his abbot had asked him to do almost anything else, anything that didn't involve leaving the abbey.

"Yes," he said finally. "Of course I will come with you. I counsel that you should leave not tonight but at first light in the morning—or by the time we're sorted and saddled, the nuns at Motherwell will be going into silence at the hour we arrive. I can make the arrangements if you wish it."

John nodded, but he looked disconnected and remote.

"Thank you. Thank you, William. I shall be myself again in a minute. Thank you. I just can't bear . . . "

William waited. Then, "I know," he said. "But if you go back into your chamber and close the door, I doubt anyone will have the temerity to disturb you except maybe Brother Michael with your physic. I will make all arrangements and come back. Father John—" John looked at him, and William met his eyes steadily. "You will get through this. I promise you. You will, with time, come out on the other side."

John nodded vaguely. "Of course," he murmured. He did not sound confident.

William left him standing there as he stepped out into the courtyard, closing the door behind him. He walked first across the court to the stables near the gatehouse, to ask for their horses to be made ready for the morning, then to the kitchens to ask Brother Conradus to prepare and pack food for the journey. After that he went in search of Father Chad.

In the abbot's lodging, John stood without moving a little while longer, and then he began to shake. Drifting like a man in a dream, he withdrew to his chamber again. He collapsed onto his bed, lying there for a few minutes before he found his way under the blankets, where he curled up in a tight ball. Overcome with cold, he shivered, even to the extent of his teeth chattering. He wished he might fall asleep but remained in a state of wide-eyed awareness, conscious of even the tiniest sound, every sensation. The agony of his soul felt as though the whole of him were racked . . . stretched . . . stretched . . . stretched to breaking, to the brink of tearing apart. He felt the ligaments and tendons of his soul snapping and tearing; he groaned and shivered, so very cold.

In this condition Brother Michael, the infirmarian, found him, having given him more than an hour's space and solitude, considering that to be quite enough time before intervening.

John heard the sound of someone open the door from the cloister but did not register the meaning of the sound. He lay acutely alert to everything; yet all of it had lost meaning. Brother Michael entered the inner chamber, moving quietly, clothed in his habitual air of gentleness. He came to John's bedside, a cup of steaming liquid in his hand, observing John's trembling and pallor. He stretched out his hand to touch his abbot's brow, but with a sudden reflexive movement John flinched away. "Please don't touch me."

"Sit up then," said Michael, quietly withdrawing his hand, "and drink this."

"What's in it?" asked John, his voice dull as he struggled to a sitting position, clinging still to his blankets.

"Well," replied Michael, gently coaxing his brother—who had taught him every healing art he knew—back into reality, "what would you have put in it?"

John tried to find the answer as he took the cup from Brother Michael's hand but said in a tone of complete hopelessness, "I don't know. I can't think."

Michael sat on the end of the bed but not too near him. "Lavender, lemon balm, rose petals, chamomile, passion flower, and a handful of oatmeal, in milk."

John focused on this soothing litany; the recital of the herbs whose uses he knew so well recalled him in some small measure to himself. "Sounds vile," he replied in a brave attempt at humor, still shivering violently.

"Let me help you with that, else you're going to spill it." Brother Michael was always kind, but he recognized the moment to be firm. "Ssh, ssh, don't shy away from me. I won't intrude upon you. I understand. Let you just take this drink, my friend, and then I'll leave you in peace. Both hands. There, that's it. Will you let me rub your feet and your hands a little? You're very cold."

"No."

In some remote external place of his being, John felt he might be behaving unreasonably. He also thought that if he could not keep everyone away from him, out of himself completely, he would dissolve into tears. And he thought if that happened, his soul would rupture completely like spilt liquid on sharp rocks. Brother Michael helped his shaking hands with the cup but refrained from touching him otherwise. "I'll find you some hot stones to warm your bed then; there'll be a fire lit in the kitchen. Lie down again now. I doubt you'll be able to sleep until I can get you warm, but rest anyway."

He tucked the blankets in around him, noting that John did not even look at him.

"Our abbot is not well," he said to Father Chad, finding him in the outer room as he left John's chamber. "I'm so sorry, Father, but you must not intrude upon him. If he has a sleep, he may be more accessible, but for the time being, he is not. Please let him be."

He placated Father Chad with the friendliness of his smile. "Thank you for coming. Thank you for your concern for him. When he is better, he will appreciate it," he added.

"But Father William is making arrangements for him to travel down to Motherwell in the morning!" Father Chad focused hopefully on another possible source of offense than himself. "It sounds as if such plans are premature and inconsiderately precipitate. Father William should not have pushed himself in!"

"Perhaps Father John asked him to." Brother Michael spoke kindly. "I think it is likely that an hour ago he will have been more together than he is now; and if he can sleep this evening and tonight, he may well be up to traveling in the morning. I am sure he will feel it a priority to go to his sister. But if the morning comes and he cannot go, we can always think again."

Brother Michael stood respectfully while the prior pondered this. Michael remained positioned between Father Chad and the door to John's chamber. He thought he would stay there while they talked.

William appeared in the entrance from the cloister. "Father Chad!" He made just the suggestion of a deferential bow. "I have made the arrangements as you recommended."

Father Chad's eyebrows rose. He had no recollection of recommending anything. Then seeing the obvious advantage if he had, he decided to grasp the proffered opportunity to appear in command.

"Ah! Thank you! Well done! We shall see how he goes on then. He may, of course, not be well enough to travel in the morning, but you can stay on hand, in case he is."

"Brother Ambrose has some bills he cannot pay without the abbot's permission." William spoke in a low, respectful voice. Brother Michael continued to stand quietly, holding the empty cup.

"What should we do, Father?" William's innocently troubled eyes sought and held the prior's. "Must we wait for Father John to recover to approve the payments himself, or would you have the authority to do that?"

"Oh, certainly I have! Yes, you don't need Father John for that!" The prior looked genially at William's submissive demeanor and respectful countenance. "I'll go right along and get those dealt with at once. Thank you, Brother Michael, for your help with the medicine. I presume that was medicine you had in that cup?"

Michael nodded, smiling. "It was."

"Right then!" William stepped back from the doorway into the cloister, and Brother Michael took one step forward. Father Chad took this to mean they were all departing and set off for the checker as Michael followed slowly out of the abbot's lodge and William latched the door behind them.

"There better *had* be some bills needing the abbot's approval or you'll be in trouble!" Brother Michael observed as Father Chad moved out of earshot.

"I don't know how you can say that," William replied. "Do you think there has ever been a day in any abbey in England when there were no bills waiting to be paid? How is he? Not good?"

"We should not be talking here in the cloister. Still, there's no one here to disturb. He is in deep shock. I'm going now to find some hot stones to warm his bed because he is shivering with cold. The best thing for him would be the release of tears. But you know, I don't think I've ever seen John weep."

William nodded. "Stick around then," he said, "because I've a feeling we very shortly will see exactly that. He is but human."

"Indeed, poor lad. Is it right that he asked you to prepare for him to travel down to Motherwell?"

"It is. He asked me to go with him."

"You have helped him a great deal, I think, in this short time. You seem to have become very close to him."

William's appearance of impassivity gave no hint of his apprehension lest John's acceptance of his company caused jealousy and antagonism, but he saw that Brother Michael felt at peace about this; he had no sense of friendship usurped. Even so, he thought it better not to allow any suggestion that he might have acquiesced to the notion of a bond of friendship developing between himself and the abbot. "I'm not close to anyone," he replied imperturbably. "Some find that repellent;

some find it intimidating. Every now and then comes a day like today when it's just what someone needs. I have no warmth. I don't attach. I'm just here."

Brother Michael smiled. "I wouldn't say you have no warmth. It's just that you only exercise it on a leash. Where are you headed? I'm going down to the infirmary now to find some stones. I'll see you later."

With the comfort of hot stones at his back and his feet, and the drowsiness of sleep herbs taking his senses under, John collapsed into something like sleep for several hours.

The hour for Vespers came and went, and suppertime. As evening fell, John found himself suddenly, searingly awake. For a fleeting instant he clung to the illusion that he had woken from a bad dream, that what filled his mind and his memory was no more than some awful story. As the recollection seeped in again that it was all true, his soul shuddered and tried to find a way back into sleep, but that door was shut now. He had no idea what time it might be. After a while he sat up in his bed, then stumbled through from his chamber into the main room of his house. The evenings still came down cold, and Brother Tom had lit a fire and now sat on the stones of the hearth, patiently waiting for his abbot. He had heard John moving in the inner chamber but did not stand up; on reflection he thought it might be more helpful to remain where he was, on hand if wanted. It went against the grain to remain seated when his abbot entered the room; even so, he thought it would suit John's current needs. John, he had perceived clearly, did not want fuss and in his present state of mind found human interaction intrusive and burdensome. Tom wondered if it was strange that a man whose life had been devoted to healing should find the touch and proximity of others so unwelcome in his own time of distress; or if it somehow was exactly because of the healing vocation.

John looked down at him. "What time is it, Brother? Thank you for lighting the fire." His voice sounded so remote, so distant.

"It's just a short while until Compline."

John nodded. "Did I . . . did I miss Vespers?"

"Father Chad saw to Vespers for you, and if you like, he can do the same for Compline."

"No. No. I'll go to Compline. I think I should."

"Can I get you some supper?"

"What?" John frowned, puzzled, as if Tom had suggested something he had never heard of before. "Supper? No. No, I don't think so. Did you say it was time for Compline?"

Tom got up. "Father—John! John! Just sit down here by the fire for a minute. Right here; that's it. Stay there now, be at peace. I'm going to find Brother Michael."

Anxiously Tom let himself out into the cloister, casting a glance back at John as he did so. He felt relieved when his abbot sank without question into one of the chairs by the fire. He sat now, staring at the glowing logs, his face preoccupied. He looked far away.

As he turned from closing the door, with relief Tom saw William, who sat quietly on the ledge of one of the arches that looked into the cloister garth. "Can I help?" He slipped down from his perch and stood ready as soon as he saw Tom emerge.

"You can indeed. Will you stay with him while I run for Brother Michael? He's not right. He says he's going to Compline, but that may not be realistic. Talk to him, maybe. He seems a bit confused at present."

William nodded and, as Tom set off with all speed for the infirmary, unobtrusively entered the abbot's lodge.

He walked with no sound across the room and sat without speaking on the hearthstone.

"That's exactly where Tom was just sitting," remarked John without taking his eyes from the fire.

William still said nothing; but he saw his abbot fractionally relax. William's presence rested John. From as far back as he could remember, Abbot John had been drawn irresistibly toward healing: and he found that, wherever he went, people's souls touched him, clung onto him. He had come to take this for granted and for the most part welcomed it as what he had come here to do. He found that power went out of him toward other people, in the form of compassion and strength, to restore wholeness. He consciously opened the channels of his heart and soul to allow the love of Christ to pass through him to the places where others seemed needy. At times this made him very tired; on this day it was simply unthinkable. Inside, he shied away in horror from the hungry touch of souls—anybody's soul, except, for some obscure reason, William's. Somehow he felt that William asked of him precisely nothing; he merely kept watch. Gratefully John absorbed the sense that with this man he was safe; not only would William desire or demand nothing at all, but he would stand between John and anyone whose need leached out his strength.

"Did you say we are going to see my sister tomorrow?" John asked suddenly.

"I have arranged that," William replied. "We can go, but we do not have to. If you do not feel well enough, we need not go. Unless you eat something before we set out, we will not go. Unless you look a lot better tomorrow morning than you do at this moment, we won't go either."

"Don't I look well?"

"Not well? You look like death. And you sound like someone in a trance."

John turned his head to look at William. "I shall be well enough to travel. I can't eat now, but I will eat in the morning. I feel as though wherever I am is out beyond the stars some-where. But I must go to Madeleine, there is no question about it. And you are coming with me?"

William nodded. "Indeed I am." He considered John's words and thought that despite the odd vagueness, his abbot was probably functioning at a workable level.

"I'm all right," said John as if William had voiced his thoughts. "Truly. It's only I feel a bit dazed, kind of pushed sideways. As if my soul has been dislocated, shoved aside by this solid enormity of pain. But I'm all right. If we go . . . if we go at the first lightening of the glory in the east . . . can we?"

"Sunrise?" Amusement gleamed in William's face. "Yes, we can go at sunrise."

"Do I sound . . . am I not making sense? Why are you looking at me like that?"

William met his abbot's puzzled gaze with affection. "You sound a little crazy, Father, and more poetic than your regular self, but nothing that is hard to understand. Anyway, here's Brother Michael now, and Brother Tom."

"I'm going to Compline," said John firmly to Brother Michael. "I am. Don't tell me I'm not. Unless . . . we haven't had Compline, have we?"

Brother Michael smiled at him. "Drink this up, Father. It's an eggnog, with some honey and herbs in it. Ssshh, don't argue; just drink it. You can't go to Compline, or go to Motherwell in the morning, if you don't drink this."

John looked at him in astonished obduracy. "Yes, I can," he said with the accurate simplicity of a child. William bent his head to hide his amusement.

"I've made it for you, Father; will you drink it now?" Brother Michael was taking on an indefinably immovable quality. His abbot took the cup from his hand and obediently drank.

"Now can I go to Compline?"

"Just wait five minutes," said Michael, tranquil, waiting. In five minutes John was asleep. Brother Tom and Brother Michael carried him back to bed, William pulling back the blankets and removing the stones, now cold. Michael tucked him in comfortably, and the three of them withdrew from the chamber.

"It's only extreme shock, obviously," said Brother Michael. "Keep the fire alight in here through the night, Tom. He's more likely to sleep through if he's warm. If he does awake, it'll likely be from a nightmare, so if you can put down a sheepskin or something and room in with him, you'll be here if he wakes. Like old times, eh? Sharing Peregrine's chamber, I mean—Tom had to be on hand for Father Peregrine, William, to help him with his clothes and shoes and everything. Did he talk to you, William? John, I mean. Was he sounding lucid?"

"Lucid, yes. Quite clear about what he intends. But he sounds odd. Voice from the realm of Weird or something. Expressing things a bit strangely."

Michael smiled. "I think he will be more himself by the morning—I sincerely hope so, and I'll be worried if he's not. It's a way of the soul buffering against what is too much to bear. Sleeping allows the inner being to come to terms enough to take the next step. And I think if he doesn't get to see his sister, he'll go out of his mind with anxiety for her. John loved his mother, and loves his sister too, very much. So long as you go with him and take care of him, William, I see no reason why he can't do this journey. He and Madeleine will be a comfort to each other. Let him sleep for now, and we'll see in the morning. And there's the Compline bell. Will you nip across and alert Father Chad to finish off for us tonight, William? Tom, let's make up this fire, then I think you should stay here with him. Don't go to chapel. I'll run to the infirmary for some skins and a blanket so you can bed down here tonight."

✠ ✠ ✠

Brother Thomas brought the old chestnut mare from the stable to the mounting block and tethered her loosely to the iron ring, while William led his gray palfrey out to a nearby hitching post.

"Father Abbot looks grim," Tom remarked. "He didn't touch his breakfast; but he's hell-bent on going to Motherwell."

"Did he not? Well, he should have. It's twenty miles to Motherwell. I have some bread and cheese and apples in our pack, and he'll eat that at midday if his appetite returns or not. It's a downward spiral otherwise."

Tom nodded. "Hunger and grief affect people in similar ways. Still, Michael's had a look at him and had a chat with him, made him have a wash and a shave and brought him back into some semblance of normal reality." He looked thoughtfully at William. "You don't look so grand yourself now I come to think on it. Are you all right?"

William was in the middle of shrugging this off as Tom's fancy when he stopped himself and said, "No." Tom smiled at this sudden breakthrough of honesty. "What's amiss?"

"Nothing more than the usual terrors. I feel safer within the abbey walls. I was on the verge of asking him to find another traveling companion, but when it came to it, I hadn't the heart to refuse."

"You?" Tom looked at him, teasing, affectionate. "I didn't know you had any kind of heart."

It was a measure of the distance these two men had traveled in their understanding of each other, laying old enmity to rest, that Tom could trust this gibe to be taken in good part.

"Thank you very much," came the sardonic reply. The exchange was not trifling, nor as superficial as it seemed. Tom knew reassurance would be needed that he took no offense from John's preference to travel with another brother. As his esquire, Brother Thomas would be the natural and obvious candidate; their abbot's choice of William—neither his prior nor his esquire—as his companion needed a reason. Tom and William both knew the only reason was that in his present state of mind it was William's company John needed, and Tom wanted William to know he understood and bore no grudge. His expression of concern and the teasing jest that went with it let William know they were still friends. William's disclosure to Tom of the vulnerability of his fear was a sign of reciprocal goodwill. The exchange seemed slight enough, but this was the currency of trust. Community cannot be built without the patient attention to the layering of such reassurances.

Brother Michael came walking across the abbey court with Abbot John, passing him into Tom's good care. John was but a shadow of his usual self. Even so he mounted his horse well enough, and Tom unhitched the reins and handed them up to him. William, sitting elegant and easy on his palfrey, had their pack of food for the journey, along with money for hospitality in Motherwell and any other necessity that should arise.

Having slept soundly through the night, John had awoken that morning with almost no recollection of how the day before had gone. He had been in his stall for Prime and presided as usual at the morrow Mass. Brother Tom thought there was no getting around it, he did look undeniably rough. But he was functional now, which was more than could have been said of him the day before. As he rode out with William, he seemed withdrawn and low in spirits but calmer. Tom saw the shrewd appraising glance with which William assessed his companion's well-being and knew that John would be in trustworthy custody.

"God keep you safe, both," Tom whispered under his breath as he watched them go. "God shield you and travel with you. Come home restored to peace, Father John."

☩   ☩   ☩

As their abbot went beyond the walls into the world, his community held him in their hearts and kept watch. They did not discuss or speculate, but their prayers brooded over him. There was work to be done, as always, but with the abbot away, his esquire found himself restless and at a loose end.

"Not often in the time I have known you would I have accused you of thinking," said Father Francis as he sat down beside Brother Thomas on the grass of the riverbank, "but I have to admit, you do look pensive now. Is something wrong, or are you just worried about our abbot?"

"No. I was fine. I was perfectly content, sitting here by myself." Tom glanced at Francis. "Actually, that just sounds rude, doesn't it? My attempt at humor. Sorry."

Francis laughed. Together they sat and watched the bright water of the river's flow—flashing silver as it tumbled over stones this high in the hills, gathering in little brown-gold pools in still spaces here and there in the lee of craggy rocks.

"D'you think we maybe have too many rules?" Tom asked suddenly.

Francis turned this question over in his mind. "We have one Rule, don't we? A way of life. To help us channel all the turbulence of what we are into something more constructive. That's what religion is."

"Yes . . . " answered Tom slowly. "I suppose so." He picked up a small stone and flicked it high, watched the arc of it falling into the bright water, where it sent a small spurt of shining splashes as it hit the surface.

"But when I was a lad," he said, "I mean, right up to the day I entered here, I would have stripped off my clothes and gone for a swim on a day like this. In the fishpond or the lake or where the river widens out as it comes into the valley. I would have got up at first light, while the mist still lay on the water, and dived in. I remember it, the amber gold of the water with the sun shining through it. Geese swimming on the lake, fish jumping, the sunrise reflecting. It felt beautiful. So alive. And then I never did it again. When would I? Every minute is spoken for. As the sun rises, we're in prayers or only just coming out. If we've finished Prime, it'll be only minutes before Mass is starting. The morning is all for work. The afternoon you can never be sure there won't be stray visitors wandering about. Everything is accounted for. Every thought is turned to prayer, every moment to industry; no wild places left. No space to play. No nakedness, no glory in what we are and how God made us. Everything is so relentlessly . . . proper. Nothing gets to be itself. It's all on purpose, patiently espaliered into the correct lines of growth for a good monk."

"Is . . . is that a problem?" Francis screwed up his eyes against the afternoon sun to see his friend's face.

"Well . . . you know . . . I guess not. Living and loving in formation. Remembering not to laugh too loud, not to whistle a tune once the Great Silence has begun. Not to love the wrong person or love too much or love too little or in the wrong way." He felt for another pebble in the earth and flicked it into the stream.

"Love?" said Francis softly. "Who?"

Tom laughed. "Don't you worry. I haven't lost my heart to a wench in the village. It feels strange though now—being John's esquire after being Father Peregrine's. It's the same, and it's all different. Waiting at table, sweeping the house, making sure his washing gets put out and brought back, fetching his firewood, bringing refreshments for his guests. Same shape to the job. But I'm not to him what I was to Father Peregrine. We get on well enough, but . . . it was William he needed at his side when these bad tidings came; it wasn't me. I'm not who he turns to when he needs someone. And why should I be? I don't mind that. He'll be a good abbot if he ever gets a chance between one disaster and another. I'm right behind him; I think he's great. And don't get me wrong, he's been good to me. But . . . how it was with Father Peregrine . . . it made sense of my vocation. Was it wrong? Was it a 'particular friendship'? I can't say. Father Chad thought it was. There were those years of traveling along with him that seemed to ask everything of me. He had such power about him, such fire. And such faith. What was in him was enough for both of us somehow. Then when he died, the agony of that parting tore me up so I could hardly think of anything else for a long time. Then we elected John, and off he went to university that year . . . came back . . . asked me to be his esquire, and why would I not? And now I'm just . . . bored or something. Life has lost its flavor. I want to go skinny-dipping. I want to go to bed with a woman. I want to laugh as loud as I like and drink too much and eat roast ox and remember what it felt like to be alive. Don't you know what I mean?"

Francis sighed. "In one way, yes; of course I do. We all get that spring evening restlessness, don't we? And we all get those gaps between the movements of life when the dance stops and everything stands still for a while. But I quite like 'boring.' I think it has its merits. What you described sounds vivid and exciting and fun, but that's not every chapter in the book, is it? Some of those men you spoke about, laughing loud and stuffing themselves with roast ox and downing ale by the yard, ended up raping John's sister and killing his mother—and personally I'd rather put up with being bored every now and then and live by a Rule that offers something better. William de Bulmer flouted every rule in the Rule, it would seem, and what happened to him? They set his house on fire. And where did he come running for sanctuary when that happened? Here, where the men are boring and apply their thoughts to the drearier things like forgiving each other and healing and turning again and again to prayer if they feel like it or not. I think I could put up with quite a lot of that kind of boring. What you're talking about is good fun until someone gets hurt.

"And it's the same with going to bed with a woman; that's fine, but if it's an honest, real relationship, not just using her, you have to marry the woman. And the same woman that took your breath away one May evening when the bluebells were shining in the dusky woods is the nagging old harridan with stringy gray hair and dugs down to her navel and no teeth, who gave you six brats you had to work your whole life to keep in porridge and shoes without holes. And are you going to tell me it would never have crossed your mind that might grow boring after twenty years of it went by? At least here when the Great Silence falls everybody has to shut up finally, which is not the lot of married men, from all I've heard."

"You've converted me," said Brother Tom with a grin. "I want to be a monk."

"Aye, good! I'm pleased to hear it. And just to rub your nose in it, it's seemed to me that Father John hasn't looked too bored with life these last couple of days. That's one of the alternatives to being bored you might have wanted a taste of."

"Thinking before I speak was never the crowning glory of my virtues," said Tom penitently. "I hear you. And I'm grateful enough for what we have. It's just . . . "

"Look, Brother, do you really think that if you slip out after Prime for a dip in the fishpond anyone will miss you at Mass or care if they do? Take a towel from the lavatorium and go for it, my friend. This is a way of life, not a ball and chain in prison! You're the abbot's esquire; he's away for a few days—why not?"

"Truly? You think I could do that? And you a priest of the church? Well, and I might just do that if I'm still chafing to be free in the morning. In the meantime I promised Thaddeus I'd help him dig some clay."

CHAPTER
TWO

*S*mall and comfortless, spotlessly clean, the parlor had been furnished with nothing at all except two stools.

Perhaps once a year the family of a Poor Clare might visit her; and when they did, the meeting would take place in this austere divided room. A door led into it from the convent side, and a door from the externs' lodge and the guest house, on the side of the world. In the wall that divided the room exactly across the center, a rectangular space four feet wide and three feet high made communication between the sisters and their visitors possible, but the iron railings that barred the space set limitations to every encounter. In many enclosed communities, the grille was curtained as well as barred. In this house they contented themselves with the railings; they were not more brazen than other religious women, but they were short of money for linen.

John and William waited in silence for their requested audience with Madeleine, seated on the two stools made ready for them in the center of their half of the parlor. William felt cautiously pleased with the condition in which he had managed to escort his superior to this meeting. The familiarity of saying Mass and the office, and the small amount of food William had coaxed him into eating when they stopped at midday, had restored a measure of equilibrium to John's shattered soul. On the journey to Motherwell, William had left John to his thoughts only a little while; then he had drawn him expertly and gracefully into conversation, eased him into discussing matters of little moment but of interest and diversion. By the time they arrived at the monastery of Poor Clares, his abbot had recovered a considerable measure of self-possession and was looking forward with impatience to seeing his sister. He loved her. They had always been the best of friends. Over the years he had been at St. Alcuin's, naturally a greater distance had developed between them; sometimes he had felt that she withheld from him thoughts she might once have spoken, but that seemed inevitable since they no longer lived under the same roof, sharing the warp and woof of every day. It was part of growing up. People drifted apart. Even still, he and she had ever been glad to see one another; he had always contemplated his little family's visits to St. Alcuin's with eagerness.

As the door opened and his sister came into the room on the convent side, John rose to his feet and went to the grille. She wore the brown habit of a Poor Clare and a postulant's veil.

"Madeleine—" he said. "I'm so sorry. I'm just so very sorry."

He put his hand through the bars to her. Though she glanced at his hand, she did not come across to the grille but sat down on the stool on her side of the room, her eyes lowered.

"I'm so sorry," he said again, his voice shaking.

Then Madeleine stared at him, remote, composed, very pale. "Yes," she replied, "no doubt it would never have happened if you had been there."

Silence followed these words. Blindly, John stepped back from the grille and sank down on the stool provided for him on the visitors' side of the parlor. He could find no means of addressing this response. Neither did William speak. In silence he observed the depth of John's distress; then his eyes turned to contemplate the woman who had caused it.

Eventually Madeleine said, "Well, it was good of you to come. I'm glad you came." But her voice had no color and no sincerity; the sentiment was produced by determined application to duty. Reverend Mother had said she must come and do this. She was trying her best.

John got up again and went back to the grille. Gripping the bars, he pressed his face against the railings, to be as close to her as enclosure permitted. "Madeleine—" he whispered. "Please . . . "

Her careful composure broke apart, and her head jerked up sharply. She fixed John's eyes with hers. She stopped trying to be what she had set herself to be and became simply herself. Her evident anger hit him like a hard slap in the face.

"*What?*" she demanded, in sudden concentrated fury. "*What* can I do? *What* can I say? Our house was burned. Five men raped me. Mother died in the fire. She was terrified and alone. We had no one to defend us. *What* do you want me to say? That it's all right? That it's over now? It will *never* be over. It will *never* be all right again. I died with Mother—and just as alone! What you see here now is a body that inconveniently lived. When I am professed, they will give me a new name; and it will be the name of this body that has no soul. Whoever Madeleine was is *dead*. And, yes, it would have been different if you had been there."

Gripped by the glaring fury of her red-rimmed eyes sunken in the pallor of her face, John stood, his knuckles bloodless as he hung onto the railings, his knees trembling, absorbing the savage power of her accusation. He had no thoughts about it. It was bigger than thoughts. It overwhelmed him. By his absence, by his preoccupation with his own vocation, he had done this, it seemed. He was responsible. That this might be true appalled him, shook him to the foundations of his soul. Had the flames, the violence, the coarse laughter, the lewd brutality, and lonely terror proceeded from the all-involving obedience of the abbacy, his full and overflowing round of duty, work, and prayer? What he had chosen had seemed holy, devout, and Christ committed, but out of it, this had come.

"I am so sorry," he whispered. "Please, sister, please forgive me."

The brief flare of anger had subsided. She had very little energy for it; it soon drained her. Now her eyes, large in her ghostly face, with none of the old laughter in them anymore, looked at him as if he were a stranger, as if she had lost the language of family and love.

"Sister?" Her tone was flat and dull now. "Yes. I will be a sister of this house. Here I will learn to forgive. I shall learn the rules that will school what was my heart until it can find a way to forgive you."

John bent his head, resting his brow against the cold iron of the railing. A nun? Madeleine? He found this hard to take in. His mind was beaten senseless, shocked beyond rational thought. Even so, her intention filled him with foreboding. He well knew religious vocation to be an uphill road that asks everything, not a healing refuge for a torn soul. The peace and safe harbor a religious house may offer those visitors who take refuge there is won at the cost of hard daily discipline and dogged turning away from the peevish demands of self on the part of the community who have made it their home. He knew his own state of mind offered little of rational assessment right now, but he judged his sister to be in no fit state for joining anything.

"Can you do this?" he asked her, his voice anxious and upset. "Dearest sister, this seems no time to be taking such a step. If you have no vocation, can you bear this life? Dear one, it is not easy."

A coldness settled over her, as though the flash of authentic response from a moment ago had hardened off. She stared at him woodenly.

"I have a vocation to find a safe refuge," she said, the words coming stubborn, bitter. "And it would seem I have a vocation to survive. The life of this house may look simple and strict to you,

but compared with the rumors and the whispering, the innu-
endo and the ostracism and the fear we have put up with for
years, it does not seem so very hard to me. It is not thought to be
easy to live in a monastery. But I tell you, compared with being
flung to the ground with my clothes torn off and held down by
my hair while five leering village peasants take it in turn to
hold my legs apart and force themselves upon me, I think I may
find it easy enough. Look at you! You don't want to hear this,
do you? You don't even want to think about it! No. Neither did
I, but I *had* to be there: I had no choice in the matter. I could
not choose to run away, or I would have done so. And now? At
least in this house, if they receive me, they will cut off my hair.
No one will ever hold me down by my hair again. If it happens
to me again, the veil will come off, and I shall be able to fight
free. Do you know how much that means? I had not thought I
had a vocation to be a Poor Clare, 'tis true enough, but I know I
am no witch, nor yet a heretic or blasphemer. And at least here
no one will spit on me because I can read the missal and scribe
the *Pater Noster*."

She let the words punish him like the knotted tails of a
lash, regarding him with uncanny, calm hostility. "Don't weep,
brother; it's too late for that!"

He did not raise his eyes to her. He rested his bent head
against the railings of the grille and suffered the guilt and horror of it all to tear at him. Blood ran down his soul.

She watched him for a while; then it was as though a shutter came down inside her. She moved one hand in a small fretful
gesture of impatience. Of what use were his tears?

"God bless you," she said, matter-of-factly. "God forgive you.
God give you good day."

She rose to her feet, lowering her eyelids as she had seen
the sisters do, so that she cut him off from her sight, and left
the room.

John, upright only because he still clung to the grille, stood there with his back to William, weeping as though his heart would break. It did break.

William still said nothing. He held his peace and waited. His watchful soul, like a bird of prey on a crag, surveyed this bleak storm havoc without a sound. Against the harsh austerity of that stone room with its dividing grille, swept clean of dust and free of any comfort or ornament, the sound of his friend's weeping was the only reality, and nothing relieved it at all. At some point the extern sister opened the door into their side of the room. Her face, already full of concern as she beheld the abbot, took on an expression of definite alarm as she found herself the focus of William's pale and disconcerting eyes. "Not yet," he said to her very softly, and she looked entirely content to withdraw. He turned back and continued his vigil, sitting motionless, his hands resting in his lap, watching John's body racked and convulsed as the iron claw of grief harrowed over and over his soul.

But the human spirit is tough. Even its storms of anguish cannot continue forever. The agonies we do not believe we could ever survive, we do. The time came when the anguish of sobbing shaking John's body from the roots of his viscera finally abated. After a while his hands relaxed their grip, and he let go the grille, turning to stumble across the room to the stool they had set out for him. Collapsing heavily onto it, he bent double, sinking his face into his hands. "Oh God . . . " he groaned, "Oh God . . . Oh God . . . Oh God . . . how shall I live with what I have done? Whatever am I to do?"

And still William waited; still he did not speak.

Then at last, rubbing his tears from his face with the back of his trembling hand, John sat more upright and glanced across at William. In another moment he found his handkerchief, blew his nose, and wiped the tears that still dripped from his chin, still trickled from his eyes and would not stop.

He groaned, shaking his head in sorrow. He had entertained no expectations of this visit, knowing only that he must come; he had certainly never imagined it would be as awful as this. Hunched on the stool, lost and broken, his head bent, he held the handkerchief loosely between both hands on his knee. The tears still trickled and dripped.

Then, "Listen," said William. "Listen to me; are you listening? Listen!"

John lifted his head. Bleakly he nodded.

"You did not do this—" He dismissed John's nod of the head and semiarticulate protest with a peremptory gesture. "No, *don't* interrupt me! Don't argue with me! You did *not* do this. Each of us bears responsibility for the life we have been given. It was no more your fault that this happened than it was Madeleine's fault because she had not provided herself with a husband to guard their home. It was not her fault, and it was not yours. It was the fault of the men who did it; and one day they will be brought to meet God's justice or—even better—his mercy.

"When I came to St. Alcuin's, I was hated because of what I did to Columba—and reasonably so. Nobody thought it was his fault for putting himself in a vulnerable position as a crippled man. Nobody thought it was Father Chad's fault for failing to defend him. They thought it was my fault because I did it. And they were right.

"This is your sorrow, but it is *not* your fault. It is the way of the world. People lend themselves to working great evil sometimes. That's how it is. We are made to be able to carry the pain of that—and to recover. But we are not made to bear the guilt. If we try to do that, it crushes us. You were not there when men raped your sister and killed your mother. But Christ was there, and he did not intervene. We can only assume he was there in her vulnerability, in their rejected chance to have mercy; and he is here now in the agony of your sorrow. But, John, I am neither a kind man nor a good man, only a practical man, and I am telling you—and you may trust this—*it was not your fault!*"

As he stopped speaking, his eyes with their pale fire fixed John's. "Do you hear me?" he said.

In spite of everything, surprising both of them, something about the furious intensity with which he was regarded unexpectedly made John smile. "I hear you," he said.

"Good! Then hear this as well. Your sister will be safe here. And these are not silly women. They will understand about outrage and pain, as well as vocation. They will not profess her unless she makes her peace with life. Right now she is so full of pain herself that she has nothing left over to enable her to touch your pain gently. Suffering isolates people. But here she is in a place where the channels of healing will be kept open for mercy and grace to flow into her. The sisters will make a ring of intercession all around her, as so will we in our turn, in our house. In time it will reach her, seep through to her. Sooner or later—probably later—it will soak through to the core of her where she has been terribly hurt. Something will touch her. Someone will get through. A change will come, and she will find her way back to living. When that happens, these things can be sorted out between you, and the bond of love can be grown back into place—not as it was before, but in a new way, because you will both be different having passed through this. But there is *nothing* you can do to rush that healing or take away the pain of the journey she must make to get there. It is between her and God. It would be presumptuous to think otherwise.

"Your mother also is safe. She is healed. The sorrow and fear of this world cannot touch her now. She is safe, John, and happy and free. Do you hear me? Safe!

"The many good times are also safe: the laughter, the caress of the breeze, the joy of the sunshine, the crooning of hens amongst the herbs, watching the garden grow and the spring come, the warmth of the fireside, the beauty of stars on a frosty night, shared jokes and shared meals—nobody can take them away from the lives that had them. They were God's good gifts, and they belong to those lives forever. They are safe now.

"What is not safe at this moment is your soul. If you are wise—are you listening, my brother?—instead of torturing yourself over what you could not help and did not foresee, you will allow the grief in you to be a simple open wound that Christ may touch and, in good time, heal. This thing happened. It has broken you to pieces. If you can find the humility to allow it, grace will also heal you: you will be stronger in the end for this, one day. This grieving is the filth and mess that turns out to be the bed of sticky clay that, if we plunge our hands into it and bring them out full, we can craft into a grail of hope. It is so. I promise you."

John nodded, half-listening, somewhat holding together. "All right," he said. "Thank you. I'll do my best." He shook his head distractedly, trying to dislodge the bewilderment of overwhelming emotion. "Well, I guess we'd better go."

He got up wearily. For a moment he remained standing as though he could not remember how to put one foot in front of the other. Then suddenly his face crumpled, and he began to weep again, holding his head in his hands, sobbing helplessly where he stood in the middle of that bare room with its two wooden stools. The latch of the door behind them clicked again. Once more an extern sister looked in, murmured her apology, and hastily withdrew.

This time William stepped briskly across the room and opened the door. He glanced along the corridor where the nun was walking away and said, not raising his voice, "Sister." Monastic life is attuned to quietness. He knew there would be no need to call out. She turned back.

Treading toward him, her kindly face full of concern, she said, "I did not mean to intrude. God strengthen you, brother, in your time of loss. Oh, may God give you peace."

William looked at her. "It's not my loss, but thank you. I

think we need to speak to your Reverend Mother, and also your novice mistress, please."

"If you will wait one moment, I'll go in search," she said. As the nun disappeared along the passage, William returned to the parlor. He assessed his abbot's condition and frowned.

"My father, you are almost hysterical," he said. "It's time to get a grip on yourself. Stop. Give yourself a break. The time of tears will be long. Look at you. Your head feels light, and your belly aches with sobbing. Hush now. Let it alone. The sorrow will wait for you."

William communicated with the world in many voices, but when he spoke in the persona of an Augustinian prior, the ruling authority of his house, he never doubted for an instant that he would be obeyed. And this was the role he found his way back to now. He placed his own dry, clean handkerchief in his abbot's hands, flicking away the sodden one onto the floor, took hold of John's upper arms from behind, and firmly steered him back to a seated position on the stool provided. "Enough now!" he said. John felt the well of grief seal off. He felt like a small boy who has been rebuked by his teacher. He also felt himself in the presence of a love like a rock that would never fail him.

"D'you want your handkerchief back?" he asked some minutes later, his voice unsteady despite his best efforts, but his face finally dried of tears. William glanced at it. "I do not."

The door on the convent side of the grille opened, and two nuns came forward to the bars. John stood up to greet them, pushing the now damp handkerchief hastily into his pocket. As John and William stepped forward, William appraised the women carefully.

"God grant you peace in your sorrow, my poor brother," said the older of the two women. Short and stout, with a face physically soft and gentle but with eyes that expressed keen intelligence and immovable authority, she came to the grille. It was her intention to take John's hands through the bars in a gesture of sympathy and comfort, but as soon as she read that might not have been what he sought, she forestalled the movement. When she stepped back to the stools on the convent side of the parlor, so did the novice mistress, a tall, angular nun with vivid blue eyes and a firm mouth in a face already etched deep with the lines of her smile. They seated themselves with dignity and composure, the brown skirts of their habits falling in folds that hid the stools beneath them completely. John also stepped back and sat down again.

"I am Mother Mary Beatrix," the first nun said, and this is Mother Mary Brigid, our novice mistress. We are all praying for you every day through this harrowing time of terrible distress."

"Thank you," said John simply. "Thank you."

Seeing that his superior had no apparent intention of adding to this, while the two nuns waited politely to hear what the men wished to say, William spoke. "I am Father William de Bulmer," he introduced himself. "I am not an obedientiary at St. Alcuin's, having joined the community but recently. I have no authority, so I was free to be Father John's traveling companion. This event has hit him hard, as you see for yourselves; for which reason only, I must be his mouthpiece now and ask you the things we need to know."

Reverend Mother inclined her head. She understood.

"Firstly, of your kindness, may I inquire what has become of the body of my lord abbot's mother? By my reckoning, even supposing your messenger came the day that you took his sister in—yesterday—this is still the fourth day Katelin Hazell has been dead. It is warm weather. Have you buried her body already, or is that still to be done?"

William was aware of John's movement of horror and distress but did not turn his head to look at him.

"We laid her in the earth early this morning." Mother Beatrix let her calm voice steady this situation as it had had to steady so many others. "It would not have been a blessing or a comfort to you to see her."

"I understand," said William quickly, sensing John's trembling and thinking it best not to linger where imagination might dwell on the implications of what had been said. "Where is she buried, please? Might my lord abbot pay his respects at her place of burial?"

Mother Mary Beatrix nodded. "Certainly. Usually only our sisters are laid to rest in the burial ground here; but Madeleine has been so consumed with the dread that wicked men might violate Katelin's grave, we made an exception. I'm so sorry, Father John. I can see for myself how hard this is for you."

John felt for his handkerchief again, his hand shaking.

"We can take you directly to the burial ground, and you may visit whenever you wish. Priests of the church are allowed inside our enclosure, as you know."

"Thank you," said William. "You have our heartfelt gratitude for stepping in as you have, and bringing some healing and sanity to a time of deep turmoil and pain. May I ask you next about Madeleine Hazell?"

"What can we tell you?" responded Mother Mary Beatrix pleasantly. Her eyes rested on William with careful appraisal, and she felt more puzzled than she usually did. She thought there was something odd about this man. His assurance and authority did not sit comfortably with his assertion that he held no office at St. Alcuin's. She thought that could not always have been the case. William de Bulmer . . . she felt sure she had heard that name somewhere before.

"She was attacked on this last Saturday evening?" William asked, and Mother Mary Beatrix nodded in affirmation. "Yes."

"She hid the next day in the woods and came to you when dusk fell?"

"That's right," confirmed Mother Mary Beatrix.

"You sent word to us the very next morning, for which we

most heartily thank you, and we came down to you the day following, being this day."

Mother Mary Beatrix nodded. "Mm-hm."

"Good sisters, please do not take my questions amiss. Madeleine Hazell had not previously come to you with intention to explore a vocation as a Franciscan?"

"No. We knew her. She and Katelin had sometimes been with us for Mass. They were here only two weeks ago, at Easter, just after they had been to visit at St. Alcuin's, I gather. Katelin was very proud of her son. She wanted to tell me how he had been elected abbot, but she said that she feared it would mean she and Madeleine should not overburden him; she did not want to be in the way at a time of year when he would have his hands so very full. So they came back home and observed the vigil at the cross with us."

"Oh, by all heaven, they would *never* have been in the way! They never . . . Oh God, help me, they are both so dear to me!"

"My dear Abbot John, I didn't mean—"

"That's all right," said William quickly. "We understand. Father, your love—for your mother and your sister both—has ever been apparent, and you made them most welcome, so I heard. It was a sensible decision to come home. No superior has time on his hands in Holy Week—or on hers."

Mother Mary Beatrix rewarded his acknowledgment that women superiors also existed with a small, wry smile.

"So Madeleine Hazell had no thoughts of a vocation as recently as Easter?" William persisted. "Then why is she dressed as a postulant today? I should judge her state of mind to be wholly inappropriate for making any such commitment."

Mother Mary Beatrix nodded. *You don't miss much, do you!* she thought.

"We thought the same," she said transparently. "The day Madeleine made her way to us, we heard her story; we washed her and comforted her, for she was very distressed. We put her to bed, and Mother Mistress here sat with her through the night, for she was frightened and kept starting awake. The next morning we sent someone to look for her goats, as she was desperately concerned about them, and they could not be found. No doubt they have found new homes in the village, and what's to tell between one goat and another if they are not your own? So we left it. That day we sent word up to you at St. Alcuin's. Madeleine pleaded with me to allow her into this community. She said she had been called a heretic and a witch, and she was afraid that if she remained here just as herself, Madeleine Hazell, somehow they would come for her and drag her out and do their worst to her again. No assurance from me would convince her otherwise. I think the experience had temporarily sent her to the edge of her sanity. Mother Mistress and I talked it over. We fully realize that as she comes to herself again—though what she is in the future can hardly be the same as she has been in the past—she may wish to reconsider this decision. On the other hand, it is quite likely that once she has been so savagely persecuted for a heretic and a witch, this may in truth be the only safe place for her. Frankly, if she wants to stay alive, she may *have* to find a vocation. When one looks at it realistically, what she said to us is probably exactly true. This is the eye of her storm; this is her only refuge. Fathers, can you understand this?"

"Oh, yes," said William softly, with perfect conviction. As Mother Mary Beatrix met his eyes she remembered where she'd heard his name before: the Augustinian, the St. Dunstan's fire. William, seeing the sudden kindling of comprehension, heartily regretted giving her his name; he wondered how it was that enclosed nuns invariably had such an uncanny knack of keeping up-to-date with everyone else's news.

Mother Mary Beatrix saw the slow flush of color in William's face and lowered her eyes discreetly, giving him a moment to recover.

"Rest assured, Father John, Father William, we shall lead Madeleine gently." The novice mistress spoke for the first time, her voice slow and soft and kind. William believed her, and John raised his head to look at her. "Thank you," he said. "Of your charity, would you take us to where my mother is buried, good sisters?"

The abbess rose to her feet, and the novice mistress immediately followed her example.

"Sister Mary Cuthbert will not be far away if you care to go through into the passageway. She will open the door to the enclosure for you, and we will take you to the burial ground."

William went to look. As soon as he lifted the latch to the parlor door, Sister Mary Cuthbert, who had been waiting on the occasion of their needing her, appeared in the clean-swept and empty passageway watched over by a statue of Our Lady, cloaked in peaceful blue, her face sweet and simple, the infant Christ held protected in the carved wood of her arms.

"Dear Mother had thought you might be wanting to go in to see our burial ground." Sister Mary Cuthbert's cheerful and rosy face beheld him soberly, clouded by her concern as she heard the request to admit them to the enclosure.

William found himself moved by a sudden impulse of intense gratitude. "I think we owe you a great deal," he said. "Without your hospitality and care, my lord abbot's sister would have been alone in her trouble. Thank you for what you have done for her, for my abbot, for his mother. Thank you for seeing that she had the dignity of Christian burial. It would not have been pretty to have to search for her in whatever remains of her home. We are grateful, Sister, more than I have words to express."

"Oh!" She smiled, waving aside all thanks. "It was nothing, nothing at all; God bless you, it was the least that we could do."

William shook his head. "No; it was not 'nothing.' And we shall not forget. You will pray for my lord abbot, won't you? This has hurt him badly. He is new to the abbacy. It is a steep path his feet are finding."

"Father, we are holding him in prayer every day. As I sit with my work in my hands, in every stitch I make, I am sewing John Hazell into the wounded side of Christ crucified with sturdy linen thread. All shall be well. The sacred heart of Jesus will be his shelter."

William bent his head in appreciative acquiescence. Behind him the door opened, and John joined them in the passageway.

"Let me show you the way," said Sister Mary Cuthbert. "Follow me."

Conscious at every step of the delicacy and kindness of these sisters, William observed the dread and distress in his superior's face as Mother Mary Beatrix and Mother Mary Brigid led them out past the claustral buildings, past the infirmary and up the steep path to the burial ground. While Mother Mary Beatrix sustained a gentle flow of inconsequential words to lighten the grim miasma of horror overshadowing their walk up the hillside, Mary Brigid contented herself with silence as she walked behind the other three. And William could feel her praying for them.

As he watched John fall onto his knees beside the new mound of earth and the simple wooden cross, the cascading larksong and clear blue of this May day seemed to William otherworldly, mocking in its brightness. John did not pray. He wept.

William and the two nuns waited in patient, respectful silence; even to them, used as they were to the slow chanting of psalms and intoned pages from the martyrology, it seemed a very long time before John staggered to his feet again and turned to face them.

"She was burned," he said, "burned, choked, terrified! How could they? How could anybody do this to her? She was wise and gentle. She was a healer. Her hands stretched out to help, to bring peace, wherever people were frightened or in pain.

Why would you—why would anybody want . . . why?" He shook his head in slow, bewildered disbelief. "What a . . . mess," he said, finally.

"Who has been notified of this?" William asked the abbess. "The mayor? The sheriff?"

Mother Mary Beatrix hesitated.

"We have taken no action," she said cautiously. "These are unsettled times. The plague was hereabouts a year back, and there have been rapid changes in tenancies of the land because of it. Beasts—even flocks in some cases—have passed from man to man. It is not as easy as it might have been even a few years ago to establish beyond doubt who might rightfully own what. Things are no longer clear. Our blessed holy Father's residence at Avignon . . . well . . . the people sometimes consider . . . these are licentious times."

Mary Beatrix stopped. If she had little to say in commendation of the Pope, then silence was best. William read her silence with no effort. They lived in days of corruption, when cynicism abounded, the celibacy of priests was compromised on a grand scale, and spiritual progress bought more than hard-won. An old woman's cottage accidentally burnt down by a raggle-taggle group of drunken men would be unlikely to be seen as cause for much concern. Even so, "Katelin did not own the land, I think? The lord of the manor will be short a rent. He at least will want to know."

"It was glebe land," said John quietly. "It belongs to St. Mary's at York."

Not one of the four of them needed to voice what was in the minds of all. If the root of the ruckus had been an allegation of witchcraft, there was evidence enough. The women could read; they knew herbs; they were healers; they lived together alone without a man and under no religious rule. It was enough. Any justice sought would be countered instantly by those with an interest to protect themselves, with trumped-up stories of spells and curses and incantations. The very authorities who might have protected her would likely drag Madeleine from her refuge and finish what coarse ruffians had begun. It would be wiser to let things lie. The walls of the monastery and a cloak of silence wrapped around her would keep Madeleine safer than the king's court or the ecclesiastical authorities or the sheriff.

His face bleak and hopeless, John turned away from the grave. There was nothing to be done; he just had to accept this. The consequence of further investigation could be the devastation of his sister's life. She had enough to reproach him for already.

"I cannot pray," he muttered. "God help me, I cannot pray." He stumbled away from the grave, glancing back at it once.

"Mother Abbess, I think we must presume upon your hospitality this one night," said William. "I must go with him to the cottage before evening today. I think he needs to see what damage was done and get a grasp of how things were. It is painful now, but what we know is ever easier to come to terms with than what we imagine. Tomorrow we will make our way home. There seems little comfort we can hope to offer just now to his sister, Madeleine."

The Mother Abbess nodded in sober understanding.

"Please avail yourself of anything our house has to offer. If there is any healing, any easing of pain that we can bring to this sickening brutality, we shall be glad of it. Do not fret for Madeleine. We shall watch over her. With God's grace we may lead her out of the place she is in now. And John Hazell has a good friend indeed in you, Father."

"He's been a good friend, in his turn, to me," William responded.

Yes, Mary Beatrix thought, *so I have heard.* But she did not say it. And she thought this might not be the best day to ask if one of them could preside at the morrow Mass if they were staying overnight.

She did have to ask though.

"Dear Mother would be glad of a word," whispered Sister Mary Cuthbert in William's ear in the tranquil moments of gathering before Vespers that evening. Glancing up, he saw her standing, waiting, behind the barred screen separating the nave from the choir. Reverencing the possibility of the reserve sacrament as he passed the parish altar, William went quick and light to see what she wanted of him.

"Father," she said in the quiet undertone appropriate to a conversation here in church, "our priest is sick, and we have nobody to say Mass for us in the morning. I was wondering . . . this is awkward, for of course I should really have asked Father John."

Her gaze, quiet, level, discreet, questioned his.

"Most certainly," he responded. "Yes, one of us will. I'll ask him tonight, to find out whether he would rather I do it. But rest assured, one of us will."

Ashamed to the living core of his soul, John admitted he did not even want to think about celebrating the Mass. He had set himself to be holding together in time for their return home, but this request caught him off guard. "I can do it," said William.

As John hesitated, wretched and anxious at failing in the duty of his office and status, letting down the reputation of his house, William added, "Look, let me do this. It's the first time anyone has asked me to preside at Mass since St. Dunstan's was razed. Do you think I haven't missed it? I'm not a shining example of the priesthood, I own it, but I'm not yet spiritually dead either."

"I'm sorry," said John numbly. "William, forgive me; I never thought . . . "

"Oh, by all the saints, I meant no reproach! St. Alcuin's is jostling with priests; what would I expect? I'm only saying . . . Just give your permission, Abbot John! Make something easy!"

And John nodded in silence.

The afternoon had been hard and painful. John had no

wish to ride through the village; he did not want to be seen or recognized. He had no desire for vengeance, no wish to search for those who had hurt his family to curse and upbraid them. He had been gone too long from Motherwell; he could make no guess now as to who among the villagers might bear the blame. He had accepted that seeking justice could stir up more than it resolved. He just wanted to see the cottage.

The monastery where they were staying perched on the hillside above the treacherous ground that became so boggy when the river flooded after spring and autumn rains. Springs welled plentifully in the earth here, so the sisters did not rely on the river for their laundry or their kitchen or their baths. They had two wells, which between them never ran dry. Even so, their house had been built only halfway up the hill, so that the rising land might protect them from the north and east winds, and the reredorter might drain through the natural filter of the earth down to the river. Their drain was not sophisticated, but, given a certain level of maintenance—digging out the sump when guests had been plentiful—it served.

The two men had ridden farther down into the valley, crossed the river at the fording place to the west, and made their way up through the wooded slopes and over the brow of the hill to the cottage where John had been born on the edge of the heath, a goodly mile out of the village.

He got down from his horse without a word, handing the reins up to William, who likewise dismounted and hitched the two beasts to a fence post. William stayed where he was with the animals, leaving John space to assimilate the scene that met his eyes.

Almost nothing remained of the cottage. The thatch and timbers had gone. Its walls had been built of stone and clay hauled up from the riverbed. Men valued stones already shaped for building. There was little left now even of the walls.

The places where herbs and vegetables and flowers grew

had been trampled, and some plants dug up and taken. The goat shed still stood, its door banging in the wind. The hen-house was gone completely—not destroyed, removed.

The house place looked so small and desolate. Blackened and charred remains of household objects—a wash pail, a stool, a bedstead, clumped pages of torn books—had been left behind. It seemed that anything still worth reusing had vanished into other lives and homes.

John stepped slowly across the garden with its pretty hedge of honeysuckle, roses, and blackberry, its small shading trees of hawthorn and elder, and came to a standstill at the edge of the scattered, burnt debris that was left of his childhood home.

William watched him pick his way into the mess, stoop, and lift out of the ashes still wet with dew a book half con-sumed by fire. John raised his head and looked back, saying something William could not catch; so he crossed the garden to stand beside him.

"A missal," said John. "My mother's missal. 'Witch' indeed! Oh God in heaven! Such cruel, gross brutality." His face, hard and drawn, turned to William. "And I know, if I take this to the sheriff or the lord of the manor or any man, he will ask me, 'What did a woman want a missal for, unless she be a witch, seeking to foul it with her own perversion?' It's crazy, William, *crazy*! And it is cruel, and it's not fair."

"The world? Aye," murmured his companion, "and we must make the best of it we can."

"They take it from the Bible," John went on, his voice shak-ing, "and they take it from the tradition of the church. They go to the texts of the Church Fathers and the book of Genesis and the Law of Moses and the epistles of the New Testament to find proof that women are pits of filth and dangerous tempt-resses, cesspools of evil. From the Bible! In Christ's holy name, William, what must God think? When he looks down from heaven and sees what we do with his book, what we use it for!

Witch-hunting and stoning and pillorying and persecuting! For mercy's sake, is that Christ's gospel of reconciliation and love? Is that what the Book of God is for? What have we done, we in the monasteries who have carefully scribed out the works of John Chrysostom and Clement of Alexandria and Cyril and Tertullian and St. Jerome and Augustine of Hippo and all the rest of them? Our young men have sat in the scriptorium faithfully copying out that every woman should be overcome with shame that she is a woman, that women are the Devil's gateway, that woman is the root of all evil, that women are especially dishonored by God and should be especially dishonored by men—and here it is! Here's the dishonor! Here's what we let our scribes write that our novices might read and our preachers might teach—and look at it! Look at the result! Oh God, Oh God, Oh God! Forgive us!"

He let the remains of the missal drop to the ground and buried his face in his sooty hands, shaken with grief. He fell to his knees, bending low, convulsed with sorrow, groaning, "Forgive us. God, forgive us."

At least that's what William, standing watching him, thought he was probably saying.

William folded his arms and waited. After about fifteen minutes had gone by, he decided enough was enough. He squatted down at John's side. He put out a hand to touch him, thought better of it, and withdrew his hand.

"Father," he said, "John—come now. Come. Set it aside. You will drive yourself mad. Perhaps the Church Fathers had heartless mothers. Perhaps they had temptations it was easier not to admit. Celibacy doesn't sit easy all the time with anyone. Best to let their ravings sink where they belong and be grateful for anything left that makes sense. Come now."

But John lifted up a face contorted with fury and grief. "How can you say that? How can you make light of it? How can you brush it aside as a thing of little consequence? Look at this devastation! See what we have wrought with our pious talk! Does this mean nothing to you?"

William listened to this. Squatting began to feel distinctly uncomfortable, so he stood up again. He clasped his hands and raised them to his face, rubbing his thumb pensively against his mouth, waiting. Over his joined hands, his calm, considering eyes regarded his abbot. He betrayed no sign of impatience or irritation, but William still thought this had better stop.

John glared up at him, possessed by his anger and distress, his face blotched red and smudged with charcoal and ashes. William said not a word. The wind blew about them, carrying the scents of summer grasses and flowers and the acrid smell of burning. Above them a curlew cried.

Nothing lasts forever.

John felt the tide of rage subside, leaving behind a deep, dragging weariness.

"I loved them so much," he whispered, "and this was such a happy home."

"Come, my lord." William reached down to help him up. "We have seen what's done, and there is no mending it. Thugs are just thugs and will always find someone to beat up. And the Church Fathers, well, even the wise and great have their follies, and the Word of God is often bent to the purposes of men. They were paid to think, and they were poor workmen. Anticipation is the chief tool of leadership—to see what we have said today will land us in tomorrow. They failed us there. But let's go now. There is no further good we can do here. It's best to let it lie."

They walked in silence across the spoiled garden. As they reached their mounts, John raised his eyes to his brother, who met his gaze inquiringly.

"Does nothing of this move you?" said John. "Does nothing in you respond and understand?"

William's eyebrows lifted.

"Oh. Yes, I think so, my lord abbot. It is not unfamiliar

ground. I have been used to living with mutters of 'their entrails should be torn out, they should be butchered and burned, evil stinking misbegotten sons of Satan.' I found it quite amusing. Um—until they actually turned on me and did it, of course. Then I was only afraid. I understand. But what's to do? The world, the church, the people—they are always like this. Sometimes it will be your comeuppance, sometimes someone else's. Tears will not alter it. But they flow, and we cannot help it. We are only human after all."

John frowned, watching him as he said this. "Are your eyes blue, or are they green?"

The eyes in question flickered, and humor entered them like a shaft of early sunlight on a winter morning. "I have no idea, my lord abbot. I've never looked into them."

John turned and mounted his horse. William handed up the reins, then jumped up lightly into his own saddle.

"Forgive me," John said before he turned his horse's head to leave. "I have been so absorbed in my own troubles, I had forgotten yours as if they had never been. I ask your pardon, William. And don't tell me you don't mind. You only call me 'my lord abbot' when something's not as it should be. I'm very sorry."

William shrugged. "I'm not touchy. You helped me when I had need of it, and I believe you always would. What more would I ask? Come, Father John, it's evening, let's go now."

They went back the way they had come, crossing the river valley and climbing the incline to the monastery of Poor Clares. The sisters had no ostler, but a man from the village did the heavy outdoor work for them. He came to take their animals back to the stable. William walked with him as John made his way into the guest house.

"My lord is the abbot at St. Alcuin's, a day's ride north and high up on the edge of the moors. He is a man of power and consequence and well connected." William spoke softly to the man as they crossed the sisters' yard to the small block of stables.

"We have been to my abbot's childhood home today," he continued quietly. "A godly woman, his mother was, and his sister too. They lived there together, Katelin and Madeleine Hazell. He loved them dearly. They have been set upon. Their house is burned and looted, his mother is dead, his sister deflowered, and she has fled. I imagine you know nothing at all about this. But if you did—if you ever have word of who did this thing—you would be able to tell them that, though my abbot is minded to let this go and seek no revenge, if one hair of his sister's head is ever harmed again, there will be such hell to pay, those men will wish they had never been born; aye, and their families too. And do not think there would be any hope of mercy or redress. Just as nobody knows what has happened to these women, so nobody would ever know what had happened to *them*—only that they would have found their journey to hell had been suddenly accelerated. And I am a man of my word. You may believe this absolutely. Thank you kindly. Water them well, but don't give the gray too much grain."

He did not raise his voice, and his manner seemed pleasant enough; and yet the man's face was pale and his hands shook as William walked away. He had stolen one quick glance into the cold and baleful glow of William's eyes, and what he heard and saw entirely convinced him.

In the guest house, Sister Mary Cuthbert attended kindly to their wants. She had heated some water for them to wash after their ride through the river valley, and some hearty soup with herb dumplings. William eyed his superior toying abstractedly with his food. "Eat it," he said, "or give it to me."

John managed a smile and an apology and addressed himself dutifully to the food he had been given.

Then they sat in the deep stone peace of the chapel, on the rough, low benches there, each with his own thoughts as the time for Vespers drew near, which was when Mary Beatrix begged a celebrant for the morning's morrow Mass.

"What about the parish Mass?" William asked her.

"God reward you for your concern, but here we have only one Mass on a weekday. It is not the same here as in an abbey with many priested men."

He nodded. "Of course. It is a privilege, and, Mother, we feel your kindness to us keenly, and we are more than grateful."

Mary Beatrix's shrewd eyes appraised him with interest for one brief moment. She liked his courtesy and appreciated his protective loyalty to his superior. She wondered if all that had reached her ears concerning this man had been true. She smiled at him.

"We are glad of the chance to do what little we can to help," she responded. She made him a small bow of farewell, then lowered her eyes and turned back to her stall to start the office.

The guest house offered simple accommodation: one long room of stone walls and bare rafters, big enough for six low wooden cots with blankets, warm but far from soft, that the sisters had spun and woven from fleeces they could not sell. The walls were mercifully free from damp this near the solstice of a dry year; even so, shafts of the morning sun always exposed an unmistakably greenish tinge. William felt relieved to find they were the only guests, and so did Sister Mary Cuthbert, seeing that most of their visitors were women.

He was glad too that John acquiesced to the sisters' leaving them undisturbed through the offices of the night. Their night proved to have disturbance enough of its own. John tossed and turned and started awake sweating. William, a light sleeper always, was there at his side when needed, and he was glad when the sun finally rose at about four o'clock.

The day found John haggard and weary, exhausted from more grief than he could bear.

William said the Mass and insisted that John break his fast with a cup of hot milk and honey, even if he could not face the fresh and fragrant bread Mary Cuthbert had set out for them.

The hired man, sullen, dour, and wary, had saddled their horses. William thanked the sisters and gave them a generous gift of money, both for their care and for Madeleine's keep.

Sister Mary Cuthbert listened to the clatter of horseshoes as they rode out, and she murmured a Hail Mary for traveling mercies, then exclaimed "Drat! I had that handkerchief laundered all ready, and I forgot to give it back!"

The road up into the hills lay wild and peaceful. The two men covered half the distance before midday without any undue haste. John remained pensive, his face set in hard lines of hopelessness, and William left him to his thoughts as they passed through farmland and woodland, by streams that sparkled over stony beds and gurgled around mossed boulders. When the sun was high and he judged the horses could do with a rest, William waited for a place with grass lush enough to offer helpful grazing, a stream low enough to lead their beasts to drink, and an oak tree with ample canopy to afford them some shade.

Neither of these animals would wander. As the men slipped down from their saddles and stretched cramped muscles, William pulled off the bridles and left them to crop the grass. He carried the pack of food Sister Mary Cuthbert had given them to where John had found shelter from the midday sun in the cool green shadow of the oak leaves.

"I am finished," said John, his voice dull, his eyes staring hopelessly at nothing. He sat slumped against the tree, with no interest in the fruit and cheese William had set out for him. "Whatever I once was good for, I no longer am. I'm completely finished."

William looked up from carefully tearing in two the loaf the sisters had given them. He stopped what he was doing, remaining motionless and silent until John's attention was caught. He could not read the look in William's eyes, but he had to listen when William spoke to him.

"No, you are not finished. When they bind your limbs with

ropes to the wheel, and you hear them urge the horses on, you are finished. When they put a bag over your head so the executioner doesn't have to look you in the eyes, you are finished. When you glance down and see the first flames curling up from the fagots and the smoke is in your nostrils, you are finished. When the man who walks toward you in the forest with a knife in his hand laughs because he sees you are afraid, you may well be finished. *This* is not what being finished is. This is you having a bad day because you feel upset and guilty about your mother and because Madeleine is as trapped in her grief as you are in yours. That's valid, as far as it goes, as a feeling." William directed his attention to the bread again and finished dividing it. "But to say you are finished is simply incorrect as a fact. You have the same skills and experiences as ever—and the same duties. Shirking your responsibilities because you are half out of your wits with grief is a self-indulgence an abbot cannot afford. Take your time to rage and weep and whatever else you have to do today—after that you must pick yourself up and carry on. One of the great challenges of being human is that long after a man concludes he has finished with life, he discovers to his dismay that unfortunately life has not finished with him. Here—take this: eat it. Eat your bread. No, truly—even if you don't want it, eat your bread. There's no way to dodge this pain, but you don't have to wallow in it. Bread has strength in it, and strength you're going to need. Eat!"

John obediently took the bread pressed into his hand.

"All right, I'm eating it!" he said as William sat watching him.

"And some cheese. And you can share this apple with me."

John ate, and he drank some of the ale they had been given. William shook out the crumbs from the cloth when their meal was done and carefully folded it away.

For a while silence reigned as the two men stretched out

and rested there by the side of the road, while their horses cropped the grass and herbs that grew alongside the track. The warmth of the day felt sleepy and still. Crickets chirped, and bees were busy among the flowers, but no more than the odd scintillas and ringlets of birdsong drifted coquettishly to beautify the languid air. A lazy afternoon.

Into the peace between them, John gave voice to something that was starting to bother him.

"What was the reverend mother's name? Faith, why can't I remember? I can't seem to . . . can you remember her name, William?"

William turned his head and eyed his abbot calmly, observing his distress as his battered mind failed to do what he wanted it to do.

"I'm not completely sure," he responded, "but I think it might have been Mary."

Trying to make this fit, John eyed him with the expression of a puzzled child. "Mary? You think? But . . . "

"Yes," said William. "Never mind. She was Mother Mary Beatrix, Father John."

The day was peaceful and sunny, and here on the edge of the wood nothing could be heard but birdsong and insects and the faint stirring of the trees. For a moment William forgot his anxieties at being away from the abbey. He lay on his back in the grass, aware that his habit was getting damp and not caring, watching the clouds pass, and thinking nothing more edifying than *Sister Mary Mildew . . . Sister Mary Mandrake . . . Sister Mary Magpie . . . Sister Mary Mosaic . . . Sister Mary Millipede . . . Sister Mary Motheaten . . . Sister Mary Meticulous . . . Sister Mary Matchless Magnificent . . . Sister Mary Might . . . Sister Mary Mightnot.* "I'm sorry, Father, did you speak to me? Yes, surely. We can be on our way just as soon as you're ready."

Both of them felt drowsy, and their muscles ached from

more time in the saddle than they were accustomed to, but the sun was well past its height and the day passing.

As they took the road again, John remained taciturn, absorbed in his thoughts. William rode beside him, making no attempt to break the brooding silence.

Eventually his abbot asked him, "Is your mother still alive, William?"

"I have no idea," William answered him calmly. "I have not inquired."

"You mean she—she might be still alive and you not know? And not care? *Your mother?*"

"Yes. Yes, that is what I meant."

William did not turn his head to look at John's wordless incredulity, though he could certainly feel it. They rode on together without speaking for another mile.

"Your mother—" John broke the silence. "You did not—do not—love her?"

"Brilliant deduction."

William knew this was discourteous and thought he had better amend it.

"She was not good to me. Neither of my parents was. We were not wealthy, but we certainly were not poor. They were just not kind people. I was often cold, often hungry, often beaten. Beaten for forgetting things, beaten for dropping things, beaten if I was clumsy with food or late or rude or inattentive. Sometimes they beat me because they were drunk or had nothing else to do. I recall one splendid occasion when I was beaten because I'd got blood on the sheet of my bed from having been beaten. And I never would know if I deserved any supper—oh, it was miserable. I've found many assets in being a man of God, but the chief of them must be the consolation of knowing that if I go to heaven then for sure I won't see either of the merciless, spiteful bullies that begot me, there."

A small, mirthless half smile twisted his face as he darted

a sideways glance at his abbot. He bent forward and patted his palfrey's neck.

"Don't look so shocked, my father. It's the way of the world. It's commonplace. You must know that."

"How long did this go on?" asked John.

"Each beating? What do you mean?"

"I mean, for how much of your childhood?"

"Oh, I see." William, quietly considering, searched back for a time when he might have been simply allowed to be. "All of it that I can remember. Somebody must have nursed me as an infant, and whether that was my mother or a wet nurse I do not know. I have no memory of it. I remember only violence. And loneliness."

John shook his head, appalled and horrified. "Did nobody at all try to stop this? Did no one intervene?"

"Not as far as I know. Why would they? What grown man or woman ever takes the side of a child? And even the child—it becomes impossible to know when blame is deserved and when it is not. You can just assume it will be woven into the fabric of everything."

A rabbit dashed across their path, zigzagging, diving into the tangle of brambles that edged the way. To their left among the trees, a heavy bird, maybe a rook or a wood pigeon, startled and flapped as it took off in flight. A small cart pulled by a mule rumbled and rattled along the way toward them, and for a short distance they went single file to pass it by.

Clouds had gathered, their shadows traveling across the rising and dipping landscape as they crossed the sky.

"I think," said Abbot John, "I am coming to understand you a little better than I once did."

"People understand me well enough," his companion replied. "A man is as his actions and choices are, not what is done to him."

"Is it as simple as that? Someone who is bullied will often

become a bully in his own turn." William turned his face aside from the gentleness in John's voice, and John did not catch his mumbled reply. "What did you say?"

"I said, you hardly need to tell me that. I've already found it out for myself. But please can we talk about something else now? Neither my character nor my mother's is edifying to reflect upon. Talk to me about your mother. Tell me about your home."

Another rabbit started right in front of them, and William's palfrey shied in alarm. John observed William as he soothed her, bending forward to whisper quietly. Her ears moved in response to his words of reassurance. Something about him told John of a well of unexpressed tenderness. An animal cannot bond with coldness or cruelty, and this palfrey was readily pacified under his handling. She trusted him.

"She's a fine creature, that palfrey of yours," John said as he watched William settle her.

"She's a sound animal, but she isn't mine."

Once he had her quieted, William spoke to her softly, and they walked on. "She belonged to St. Dunstan's before and to St. Alcuin's now. I cannot call her my own."

"Oh, *I* agree with you, but I'm not sure *she* does."

William heard this but would not be drawn. "Tell me," he said again, turning his questioning gaze in his abbot's direction. "Tell me about your family and the life you lived at Motherwell."

In the presence of one whose own upbringing had been so bleak and starved of love, John hardly liked to reminisce on a childhood home that had been a cheerful sanctuary of kindness. But William seemed composed, unmoved by the memories of his own childhood.

For the rest of their journey home, John relived the past. To his surprise, he found that the recapture of what had been wholesome and good brought him comfort and a measure of peace. It restored a sense of sanity and ordinary well-being. He felt his equilibrium begin to reestablish.

William listened to him without interruption, neither affirming nor commenting, just letting the comforting recollections do their healing work.

As the hooves of their beasts clattered on the cobbled expanse before the abbey gates, John felt drained and weary but no longer as bruised and fragmented as he had felt before. "Brother, thank you for your wise care of me; you have done me good, and I am indebted to you. God bless you," he said as Brother Martin swung open the great gate for them and they rode in. "Thank you, Brother Martin!" he called as they swung down from their saddles. "It's good to be home."

William made no reply to his abbot's words, but as he took the reins of their mounts and led them away to their stable, his face was content. He had managed what he had set out to do.

Chapter
Three

I have brought our abbot back safe if not exactly in one piece."

Brother Michael turned, his face concerned and attentive, finished drying his hands, and hung the linen towel neatly on the rack to air as he came to listen to what William had to say. "Tell me more."

"It was not a happy visit, nor did we expect it to be, but ... the dam broke at any rate. I would never have believed a man had so much water in him, and—" William broke off suddenly, and his expression changed. "Dag nab it! I left one of our handkerchiefs on the floor of the Poor Clares' parlor. It was very wet." He frowned, irritated with himself. Linen was not for throwing away.

"Madeleine ... how did she seem? She and John—they were a comfort to one another?"

William's short, hard laugh of derision dispelled this line of thinking. "No. He could not comfort her, and she would not comfort him. Far from it. She held him responsible."

Michael's face puckered in bewilderment. *What?* His mouth silently shaped the word.

"Aye. Because he was not there for them, so they were two women alone. For sure that did not help their cause, but that's the way of the world. Nay, the violation and fear and grief had all turned outward in fury and resentment. It was not a good meeting. She reduced him to something very small and soggy indeed. That, with his own grief beside, almost annihilated him, I think. I have done what I could to put him back together, with assurance that he is not to blame and a certain amount of stern talking to on the way home, stressing that the community needs him and weeping has its time but has an end. Seems hard, I know, but I think he was on the point of dissolving. A man needs some iron in his soul to stand upright in some passes. He needed a break from his anguish, I thought. I hope I've done right. Be that as it may, he's well weary, and as disinclined as when we went away for human company. But he has returned resolved to stand steadfast and put in hand the work that waits for him here. We should keep watch, though. He has been in torment that has flung him about until he hardly knew who he was anymore. He has been entirely distraught. He may master it, but then again it could overwhelm him. We'll have to respect his need for privacy, but mayhap he should not be left too much alone."

Michael nodded thoughtfully. Then, as these words sank in, he glanced sharply at William. "Are you . . . you're not thinking he might despair of life are you?"

William did not reply, and Michael answered his own question, shaking his head emphatically. "Oh, no. No, no! John would never attempt to take his own life! He is a man of God, a man of faith. He would hold such a thing—well, we all would— as serious sin! He would not even permit himself to contemplate it, whatever life threw at him, whatever depths he plumbed. He—Oh God, have mercy—William, I'm so sorry!" Michael stopped short, flushing red in embarrassment. William's own self-inflicted brush with death had been completely driven from Michael's mind by his present concern for their abbot. "I am so sorry," he said again.

William shrugged. "No matter. It's not me we're thinking about. And I'm sure you're right. And moral fortitude was never my strong point. I make no claim to it. I am a coward, and I am used to sin, and our abbot is not: he has a sturdier soul than mine. This will not get the better of him, where it might have finished me—if guilt and family love had ever much concerned me, I mean, which they did not. Besides, an infirmary is the place for watching folk suffer. I cannot imagine but Abbot John must have had enough opportunities to consider how best we might make space in our souls for pain and sorrow."

Michael looked at him anxiously. "William, truly, I ask your pardon for my insensitivity." He moved to kneel, but with the sudden speed of an arrow William's hand shot forward to detain him, grasping him firmly by the arm.

"Brother Michael, I beg you, do not kneel to me. I cannot bear it. There is nothing to confess and nothing to forgive. I take heart to see that my own failures of courage had completely slipped your mind. Please stop thinking about me. Keep your mind on Father John. His plight is what we're talking about, not me."

He released his grip, but cautiously, acknowledging Michael's compassionate grin with a dismissive shake of the head.

"He will try his best," Michael asserted. "John always gives of his best to any endeavor. Our part will be to trust him and have patience. He will surely weather this storm. It grieves me to hear of the way things went with Madeleine though. Was it still so when you left? Did she not soften toward him?"

"We saw her but the once. I think, to be honest, he was afraid to ask to see her a second time, as so would I have been. He did not have the heart for another drubbing, and I would not have recommended it if he had. The thing's still a fresh wound in both of them. Besides, Motherwell is within a day's ride, and in time the shock of this will subside. They've been close and good friends until now, so everyone tells me. Sometimes these things harden into lifelong estrangements, but there's good hope she may come through to a kindlier view of him than she held in the encounter of these last few days."

Brother Michael considered these words. "God grant it be so. It would break his heart to lose his sister's kind regard. But you're right; the griefs we think we shall never come to terms with, in time we do learn to live with. Well, and Father John has said often enough himself in this infirmary, people are but simple really. Whatever befalls anybody, so he thought, if you can reassure them they are safe with you, keep their bowels moving, and find them something they enjoy eating, they will sooner or later come around. So"—Michael smiled—"provided we ensure he has evacuated his bowels and we feed him such delicacies as take his fancy, he's safe enough in these walls, in this community; in time he will heal."

Brother Benedict appeared in the doorway, clearing his throat discreetly in advertisement of his presence. "When you have a moment, Brother Michael . . . "

"I beg pardon, Brother Benedict! I've left you with that poor soul waiting for his ointment! Is that all, Father William? Yes? I'm sorry to hear how it went, and I'll do what I can. Thank you for your good care of him. He will mend, I have no doubt of it, but for sure he will need our patience a good long while, as well as our prayer."

Later in the novitiate Brother Benedict recounted to an intent audience what scraps he had gleaned of this exchange.

"Brother Michael looked quite downcast, and Father William seemed mighty fed up as well. I think it was about our abbot, and they were saying the journey had not brought comfort or any kind of peace. It sounded as though Father William was telling Brother Michael that someone was angry with Father John, but I don't know why or what had happened. His sister, I think. Anyway Brother Michael finished by saying we must be patient while Father Abbot becomes more himself again and pray for him as we wait. And Brother Michael said that Father Abbot himself had always thought if a man keeps his bowels open and has appetizing things to eat, he'll get bet-

ter from most things given time. I wonder if he'll come to chapel tonight and tomorrow, or if we'll still have Father Chad at
Chapter in the morning."

"Were you listening at the door?" demanded Brother Robert,
not usually held up as an example of ethical rectitude himself,
but assailed by twinges of jealousy that Benedict's position in
the infirmary secured him the center of attention.

"I was not!" Brother Benedict responded with indignation. "You can't always help overhearing what's said, can you?
Besides, nobody made you sit here and listen to it yourself!"

Brother Robert could think of no answer to this and was
relieved when the talk turned to a discussion among themselves as to what the snatch of conversation Benedict had
heard might mean. Those who had glimpsed Abbot John about
the place on the day he left (none of them had seen him since
his return) offered gloomy predictions of slow recovery. Only
Brother Conradus said nothing, but listened to his brothers, a
look of slow determination hardening into resolve in his gentle
dark brown eyes. He had duties in the kitchen during the afternoon. Brother Cormac wanted to sort through the last of the
previous year's apples up in the store and needed Conradus to
take responsibility for preparing the supper. He slipped away
from the company of his brothers' recreation in the novitiate
and made his way unobtrusively but purposefully along to
the kitchen, deserted now in the early afternoon. Nobody else
would come in until after None.

He scooped out flour from the big crock and fetched three
brown eggs from the bowl in the pantry; one still had a tiny,
fluffy, brown feather attached, which Conradus took a moment
to marvel at. So soft. So light. So impossibly downy.

He nipped quickly into the garden and selected with care
just the growing tips from the nettles and sorrel in their patch.
He paused only briefly to watch the wren go to her nest tucked
under the eaves. Back in the kitchen, he chopped his herbs

finely and made the pastry with deft, economical movements, using water cold and fresh drawn from the well. While it rested, he lit a fire of sticks in the bread oven—hot and fast was what he wanted on this occasion. As the oven heated up, he went for cream out of the cloth-covered bowl on the stone shelf of the dairy built against the north wall. He gathered it all together with focus and speed: he was ready to make his miracle in pastry.

Just fifteen minutes in the hot oven was all it required, and then Brother Conradus paused to inhale the aroma and appreciate the glorious golden perfection of what he had created. It was a profound relief to him that he met no one in the cloister as he carried his fragrant gift of love and restoration along; he would have been so disappointed to be turned back now.

Abbot John crossed his room to answer the knock. Weary beyond measure, he had no wish to see anyone. All he wanted was to be left alone. He knew that from somewhere he must find the strength to begin again, to take his mind off his own sorrow and find a generous heart in loving those who needed him once more. He was not sure how he would do that. At the moment it felt beyond him. He did not want to open the door, but he did it.

On the threshold, definitely quaking, stood Brother Conradus carrying something wrapped in a cloth.

"Come in," said John kindly, he hoped, if not enthusiastically.

With a look of determination, Brother Conradus intruded himself into this space of palpable pain. He went to the table and set down what he carried.

"I made you some of those little tarts you especially like, Father," he said, "with sorrel and nettles in a savory custard."

John nodded and willed his features into a smile. The two of them looked at each other. "Thank you, Brother," he said.

He expected then that Conradus would have the sensitivity to withdraw. But the young monk, though he would no longer look his abbot in the eye, obstinately stood his ground.

"I'm sorry, Father," he said. "I have two brothers and three sisters, and I well know what it is to long to be left in peace. And I know the look on the face of somebody who needs to be left alone. But the only thing is—how will you ever know how much we love you if we cannot come near you? We have to bother you a bit to let you know how much we care."

With great courage, as time passed with no reply forthcoming, Conradus stole a glance at the other man's face and was startled to see that his abbot looked completely mortified. Before the novice could think of any good means of stopping him, John got down on his knees before him and kissed the ground at his feet.

"I confess my faults of ingratitude and self-absorption," he said humbly, "and I beg your understanding in this difficult time. Please pray for me. I ask forgiveness of God and of you, my brother. Please be patient with me."

A terrible feeling came over Brother Conradus. He felt as though his chest had contracted and his scalp had shrunk. His belly filled with wild panic. His mouth went so dry he couldn't speak. He had absolutely no doubt that if anybody chanced upon this scene and asked any questions, they would despise him utterly for troubling his poor superior with his trifling stupid pastries in the poor man's hour of grief. And as these thoughts assailed and condemned him, his abbot waited, kneeling on the ground as every monk must until his brother—whoever he may be, even the newest novice—absolve him of his sin with honest forgiveness.

Then Brother Conradus found his second wind. He thought what he wanted to say might be too impertinent to be countenanced. He wondered briefly what his novice master would think and wished Father Theodore, whom he trusted implicitly, had been on hand to ask. But there was nobody but himself and his abbot, kneeling ashamed and contrite before him, waiting to be forgiven.

"John," said Brother Conradus, and all the love he surely felt was there in his voice. "John who loves to heal—of course God forgives you, my brother, and so do I, with all my heart. John, please come back to us."

Hindsight is a wonderful thing. When Conradus said that, with his characteristic kindhearted sincerity, he had no idea in his mind at all of a likely outcome. He certainly hadn't expected to make his abbot cry.

"Oh, for heaven's sake, shut the door!" said John, tears pouring down his face as he stood up. "I'm sorry, I'm really sorry, I can't help this; it's not like me, but it's just how I am at the moment. No—please—it's not your fault; every little thing knocks me off balance."

Conradus hesitated. "Did you mean shut the door with me outside it or inside it?" he said uncertainly. And then despite his tears John began to laugh.

"Oh, for mercy's sake, inside! Look, I'm so sorry, I didn't mean to subject you to this. Come and sit down for five minutes. I am so sorry."

He turned and led the way to the chairs by his hearth and fumbled for his handkerchief to restore some order to his running nose and tear-stained face. Conradus joined him but picked up the plate of crisp, golden tarts cooked to perfection and brought it with him. He took off the covering cloth. They smelled wonderful.

"Please just try one," he begged. "It'll make you feel less wobbly if you eat properly." In saying this, Conradus was merely echoing a belief held firmly by his mother; but he had never known her to be wrong. Brother Conradus could imagine no circumstance of life, no matter how bad, that could not be comforted by a nice cup of chamomile tea and a light snack.

And John, penitent, accepted a pastry. It was delicious. He ate two more. And he could not help noticing that though nothing had changed—his mother had still been savagely murdered, his sister still seemed to have shut him out of her heart—the simple, friendly companionship of this young man, and the delectable little pastries he had so lovingly made, did make a difference. John did feel comforted.

For maybe twenty minutes Brother Conradus sat chatting to his abbot, feeding him his works of art conjured out of wild sorrel, the tips of nettles, butter, fresh-milled flour, crushed peppercorns and salt, and cream risen from yesterday's milking, and he watched John being led slowly out of complete despair into something that could be called neither contentment nor peace but was an observable improvement. He talked to him about the kitchen garden and all that had flourished there, how the long cold winter and the slow wet spring meant the cherries would be especially good this year, now that the warmth had come. He talked to him about the infirmary and how he'd had a run on cinnamon eggnog with heather honey, which the old men liked so much that Brother Michael had to ration them to one a day in case they got too fat for him to lift. He told him about the morning he had helped Brother Mark capture in a linen bag a swarm of bees that had gathered on a low bough of the old yew tree—the one by itself down by the river—and how scared he had been of the bees but determined not to let Brother Mark see at all. And all the time as he prattled away comfortably, he watched John's face; then when he judged he had managed the change he'd hoped to try for, he sat forward in his seat and said, "It's been grand to have the luxury of a chair, Father, and I'm more grateful than I can say for you giving me your time like this when you have so much on your mind. I'll let you be now; but you'll stay with us, won't you? It's . . . it's a decision to slip down the black pit or not; it doesn't just happen."

He said this in the same peaceable conversational tone as the rest of the quiet flow of talk he had poured gently over his abbot, but John raised his eyes to him, considering those words.

"Is it?"

"Yes," Conradus asserted simply. "Truly it is. I know it is. Our griefs and sorrows, our dark night—they are like a well. And whether to fall down it or whether to draw upon it as something of value is a choice we make. My mother told me this, and I have found it to be true."

Despite the intensity with which his abbot regarded him, now that it was said, Conradus did not feel nervous anymore. *This is only John who loves to heal and needs my help*, he told himself.

John nodded slowly. "I think my mother would have said the same," he said.

"Well, there you are then. She might still guide you through this. Maybe you haven't lost all of her after all. Perhaps it's still possible to be the lad she would have been proud of."

"Oh, don't! Please don't! You'll set me off again. But I do hear you. And please pray for me; I'll be doing my very best."

"I pray for you every day," said Conradus shyly. "I always have, ever since I entered. Actually, it's not just me. I think we all do."

He took his leave then and set off with all haste to the kitchen, a little bit worried lest he had stayed too long with his abbot and left himself without the time he needed for the supper preparation.

He set to work peeling onions and meticulously washing leeks of the mud that got into every fold and crevice. The dried peas he had soaked and boiled already. He hurried into the garden to gather fresh herbs and took the time to close his eyes and inhale the fragrance of marjoram, rosemary, thyme, sage, and bay. Especially the bay. He held a leaf between his fingers, using his nails to puncture the hard surface and release the scent from the veins of the leaf. Conradus thought the God who made anything smell so glorious could be trusted to heal and renew good hope in anyone; then he recalled himself to what he was supposed to be doing and hurried back into the kitchen.

He took the slotted ladle with the longest handle and carefully scooped out the poultry bones from the kettle of stock that he had left to simmer over the embers the previous night, after skimming off the hardened fat that had congealed on the surface as it cooled through the day. This he scraped into a smaller pot, in which he would sauté the field mushrooms he'd picked last week and left drying in the pantry.

There was plenty of bread from the morning's baking. Later he would apportion butter from the big bowl into the smaller dishes to set out on the table. First he must light the fire, because it took a long while to bring the stock back up to a boil.

He did all this mindfully and methodically. Conradus put all of his soul into his cooking; it was his heart song to God.

Once he had satisfied himself that the fire had taken well and he could put his attention elsewhere for a while, Conradus thought he should check the progress of the goat's curds dripping into a bowl in the pantry. He intended to set aside the whey to make scones for tomorrow's midday meal and planned to shape the curds into small cheeses rolled in pepper and oatmeal. He had used nettles in starting the cheese, and they added a pleasant green flavor of their own.

The cheese was doing well but had a way to go yet. In the morning he would be expected to be at his studies in the novitiate schoolroom, which probably meant handing over responsibility for the midday meal to Brother Cormac. Conradus thought it would be wise to have his pepper and oatmeal mixed in anticipation of this, and left with written instructions.

He needed to grind some pepper for the soup anyway, so he thought he'd do it all at once, which was quicker than two smaller lots.

He measured out a goodly amount of black peppercorns: these were valuable and not to be wasted. It was quite a luxury to use this amount just as a garnish for cheese, but Conradus thought the delicious blend of flavors would be appreciated. He wanted to make a poultry marinade as well, and a dressing for the salad leaves they would serve with the cheese and scones; and all of this must be done today and set aside for Brother Cormac's use in the morning. He took the larger stone mortar and half filled it with peppercorns, then took it to the lower of the two tables, where he set to work briskly pounding expertly and rhythmically with the pestle.

He reflected with satisfaction on the acquisition of goats' milk as he did this. The community's cows gave enough for their own use with surplus to sell, so they had no need of keeping any other milk animals. Besides Brother Stephen had no fondness for goats, regarding them as troublesome beasts needing constant watching. So goat's cheese did not often come their way, which Brother Conradus regretted. He liked its piquancy and considered the light, tangy taste to be pleasing to the palate and a perfect foil to oatcakes or newly made bread.

This batch Father William had brought to the kitchen, having taken in it lieu of rent that a tenant could not pay. It did not cover the deficit. Neither lenient nor harsh, William simply assessed that (by the look of her) she would have no means to make up arrears, so there would be little point in carrying the debt over. The abbey was a merciful landlord, and neither Brother Ambrose nor the abbot wished to see the poor woman homeless; so William asked her what she had if she had no money. She had brought some herbs, a pot of honey, and the morning's milking from her goats. He satisfied himself with that and wrote off the remainder. The woman had been relieved and grateful and sought to bless him for his kindness, at which William looked surprised and faintly irritated.

"God bless you, good Father!' she exclaimed. "God will reward you for this kindness! Your reward will be in heaven, Father, sure it will!"

William looked at her. Neither kindness nor reward had been in his sights at all. He wanted the money *now*, and if there was no money to be had he would have to take what he could get. That was all. Had this been St. Dunstan's and he still its prior, he would have turned her out of her cottage without a second thought. He found her gratitude both unwelcome and uncomfortable.

"Be sure you get your situation sorted out by Michaelmas. Thank you for this," was all he said. He brought the pail of milk across to the kitchen himself: "Can you use this?" he asked.

"Oh, wonderful! Goats' milk! God reward you! That's welcome indeed!" Conradus swooped upon the snow-white milk with delight, and William marveled that the merest glance at the pail was enough to tell Conradus what he had—he needed neither to inquire nor taste it—the color was enough. He felt uneasy with this expression of gratitude as well: it seemed beyond justice that God should reward one man twice for the same pail of goats' milk, especially as it hadn't come because of his effort in the first place. It crossed his mind to say as much, but he thought it might be too complicated to explain his train of thought, so he simply said, "She'll need her bucket back. Don't get it mixed up with ours. Here's honey and herbs too. I hope you can use them."

Contentedly Conradus pounded the peppercorns into a coarse powder, not too fine. The fiery, crunchy little pieces that escaped complete pulverizing made the perfect foil to the fresh flavor and crumbly consistency he was aiming for with the cheese. He stirred the half-ground pepper around in the mortar and continued to pound it.

As he worked, though he watched carefully to ensure he achieved the right consistency, his mind wandered from Father William to Brother Cormac, who would be along in a while to prepare the supper with him. Both of these men puzzled him, and of both of them he was more than a little afraid.

He found William's manner terse, aloof, and chilly, and enigmatic, too. As a novice, Brother Conradus had little to do with the solemnly professed brothers in their separate world of full commitment to the order. But as a kitchener he worked closely with Brother Cormac every day and frequently encountered William, who had reinstated the required regular counting of the cutlery and inspection of the kitchen furnishings and implements. Brother Cormac usually went across to the checker with orders and lists, happy to leave much of the cooking to his capable novice, but Brother Conradus had plenty of opportunity to observe Father William when he came to the kitchen with word of deliveries or, in the case of small packages, brought them over himself.

Conradus saw the unreachable spirit, the shield of irony in William's eyes that were the color of the North Sea on a winter's day. He saw the tension in William's body, taut and quick like a fox and as cautious as a hunting cat, and he found no place for connection, no small welcoming chink that might permit any kind of friendship to establish.

But he had also observed William in conversation with their abbot and had seen a change in him then, as though an opaque screen drew back, revealing both love and respect and also an indescribable softness that Conradus would not have imagined was there if he hadn't seen it with his own eyes. It was certainly not evident when William looked at Conradus.

In Brother Conradus's opinion, Father William was alarming, and so was Brother Cormac. Chiefly what he feared in Brother Cormac was his legendary temper. Cormac himself would have been more startled than amused to know he had this reputation; "mildly irritable at times" is how he would have described himself. But tales and reminiscences had worked their way down to the novitiate, ascribing to the kitchener a volcanic predisposition to uncontrollable rage. The fact that Conradus had seen no sign of it thus far made that buried layer of molten fire even more terrifying to him. How might one know what would kindle the smoldering wrath to a blaze? How vulnerable would he be if he unwittingly broke open the door that kept the savage beast confined until now in Cormac's more or less stable exterior?

Certainly Brother Cormac could be irascible when the pressure was on, but that was normal in a kitchen. Brother Conradus expected, and got, peremptory instructions. He understood that; the work was hot and fast and complicated and had to be accurate. It brought out whatever was there in people. But so far he had seen no glimpse of the volatility he had heard about in Brother Cormac in connection with the previous kitchener, an old man who had died some time ago, whom it was said Cormac loved and fought and once had hated. Even so, Brother Conradus thought it well to keep a long way on the right side of Brother Cormac.

Because of this, a nagging anxiety clouded the afternoon. He had asked no permission to make the little savory tarts for his abbot; he thought it likely he would have been denied permission if he had asked, so he did not. Other people, he noticed, so often failed to grasp the almost magical power of food to comfort and restore, especially if they were indifferent cooks themselves. The ingredients he had used were plentiful, but he had no business to be making anything at all without permission—frankly, that was theft. He felt glad he had done it, but he also knew he would have to confess it; and if he faced the prospect with courage, he knew that it must be to Brother Cormac, not Father Theodore, that his confession be made. This gave him a bad feeling in his belly. He was frightened. He tried to console himself with the reflection that he could expect to have the kitchen to himself for another half hour, in which he could enjoy seasoning the soup to the peak of perfection; but he still couldn't help feeling jittery.

The pepper being now exactly as he wanted it, Conradus

thought he would take it to the pantry and leave it there out of sight of Brother Cormac. He wanted to make the salad dressing and mix the pepper with the oatmeal, but he wanted to oversee the proportions and mix his ingredients gradually. He thought at this stage things would go better without Brother Cormac's interference, but he had no authority to say so. He must manage the outcome with prudent circumspection.

He laid the pestle down on the table and, on his way to the larder with the pepper, remembered that he needed to put some in the soup. He retraced his steps, carrying the heavy stone mortar across to the kettle of soup, which gave off a promising aroma as it began to heat up. The soup kettle was large and very stable, standing on its own legs over the fire in the pit beneath it. Conradus rested the stone mortar on the rim of the pot, holding it steady with his left hand while he took a small handful with his right to sprinkle into the broth.

As he did so, Brother Cormac entered the kitchen with a quick, light step (even the way he walked sounded impatient), glanced across at the novice balancing the mortar on the edge of the soup kettle, and said, "What the devil are you doing it like that for?"

Already nervous of Cormac's arrival, Brother Conradus started violently, his hand shook, and the balanced mortar tipped and slid neatly into the soup, taking down with it enough pepper to ruin upwards of five kettles of broth. The wasted expense of the luxury of the pepper and the prospect of the entire community doomed to eat the soup for supper hit Brother Conradus simultaneously with such force that he did not even notice the greasy liquid dripping down his linen apron and coating his hand. The color drained from his face.

"Sorry, did I startle you?" Brother Cormac came to stand at the side of his motionless novice. "What's the matter? What did you have in there?"

"About four handfuls of ground pepper." The toneless horror in the novice's voice, the pallor of his face, and the fact that he had begun to tremble made it clear to Cormac that this was very bad. He looked at Conradus with sympathy.

"Never mind. It'll be a bit spicier than usual, that's all."

Conradus shook his head. "It'll be unfit to eat," he said.

Cormac shrugged. "Well, we don't have that option. That's what's for supper. We can't just waste it. What did you want all that pepper for anyway?"

Brother Conradus knew that such a significant quantity of something so expensive must not be taken twice. The cheeses for tomorrow could be rolled in the oatmeal and maybe chopped herbs, but replacement pepper would be entirely out of the question. And then there was the other matter. Slowly, still uncharacteristically pale, like a man in a dream, he turned to face Brother Cormac. Cormac took two hasty steps back. It would not be the first time one of his brothers in community had hit him. He felt greatly relieved, though surprised, when his kitchen novice fell to his knees before him.

"I confess my fault, Brother Cormac." The novice was unconsciously wringing his hands, consumed by his dread. "I made Father Abbot some sorrel custard pastries to comfort him because he hasn't been eating; and as well as that, I ground all that pepper to make a crust for the goat cheese for tomorrow."

Cormac waited. Nothing else seemed to be forthcoming. "Er . . . thank you," he said. "So . . . what have you done wrong?"

This experience was a complete novelty to Cormac. Though he'd had more occasions than he could count to beg forgiveness of his brethren, on not one solitary occasion had anyone seen the need to beg Cormac's pardon for anything during any of his years in monastic life. He gave more offense than he took. There had been a moment, years ago, with Brother Andrew— but even then, Andrew had not knelt before him; he just said he was sorry. Cormac had never given the matter any thought; it had certainly never occurred to him that when someone finally

did kneel in contrition and beg his pardon he would be unable
to identify a reason.

"The pepper," mumbled the novice, "and the other ingredients. I didn't ask permission, in case you said no. It was a
disobedience. I should have asked. And such a waste, too. Such
a dreadful, dreadful waste."

Brother Cormac began to laugh. "Oh, mother of God, that's
what the stuff's for, isn't it? Look, get up off your knees. No,
I'm sorry, what I mean is, if you have offended, which I cannot
see you have, then God forgives you, my brother, and so do I.
Nay, don't distress yourself; get up. There now, come and sit
here for a minute, and tell me about Father John. Did he eat
what you made him? Yes? Well, there you are then. If I had said
no—which I doubt—I'd have been wrong, wouldn't I? God bless
you, none of the rest of us have managed to get past the wall
he's built around himself; it's well done if you got through. What
was it you said you made for him?"

Conradus told Brother Cormac about the little pastries,
and that Father Abbot had seemed not eager to be disturbed
but they had talked a while. When he looked back on what
had passed between them, it seemed intensely private; to even
think of relaying it to another would be a betrayal.

"He asked that we should pray for him" was all Conradus
volunteered. "And I said we would, and we do."

Brother Cormac read from the young man's hesitation that
there had been more to the conversation than he was willing to
say, but he had no wish to pry into what he sensed must have
been vulnerable territory.

"Sounds as though you did well," he commented. "Anyway,
change that apron and wash your hands, and let's crack on
with the supper. Best we say I made the soup. They'd never
believe otherwise anyway. Tip some milk in it: that might
calm it down."

If he had sinned, then sitting through the evening meal

watching his brethren struggling through their soup was penance enough for Brother Conradus. He felt ashamed of his cowardice when later, as the servers brought through the dishes, he heard Brother Thaddeus say, "Your turn to cook this evening, Cormac?" and Brother Cormac reply, "What of it? You've had good food, and I'm sure you feel you've had plenty. Come and take a turn yourself if you can do better."

But he thought somebody must have got Brother Cormac all wrong. The warmth of kindness in which he had found himself wrapped had been palpable, for all it was casual and unsentimental. Yes, he could imagine that Cormac might be capable of firing up too quickly and speaking in haste, but he knew for sure that he would never be afraid of him now. Perhaps the cheese and the pepper and the soup were a worthwhile trade after all.

Brother Conradus had a feeling, as he trod quietly with his community into chapel for Compline, of something in a wider dimension slipping into its socket. This day had held fear and grief, with weariness, anxiety, disappointment, contrition, and tears. But where men suffered, they had been lifted up by ordinary kindness, not by saintly men but by brothers as flawed as themselves who were willing simply to be kind and to try to understand. As the day ended and night folded the abbey down into the Great Silence, its rhythms and the way it chose to follow made absolute sense to Brother Conradus. He was, he thought, in the place where he wanted to be.

The stillness of the abbey's night could discover a man's terrors. In its deep, dark hours, the souls within the silent stone walls found themselves taken down, down with the whole of the natural world into the little death of the small hours.

Getting up for the first office of the day at two o'clock in the morning was a discipline that took everything a man had. Strange, then, that the brothers knew this as a precious time, when the naked soul wrenched from sleep in the womb of night touched God in a way that had no parallels in the liturgies of the daylight hours. The remoteness of sleep still upon them, as the watchman took the lantern around to ensure that none began to doze, the murmur of plainchant rose and fell against the thick endometrium of dark, a beating heart of prayer that never ceased, never went off duty.

It was during the night, when all conversation was prohibited, that men had their wrestling Jacob moments: when they struggled, when they knew how bruised they'd been, but also when they were healed.

Oftentimes when they gathered again for the daybreak liturgy of Lauds, a brother would seem different from the man they'd seen tread quietly out of chapel after Compline, his face shuttered and defeated as he trudged wearily up the stairs on his way to bed. The God of stars and arcane transformations would have met with him in the difficult passage of the night and pressed a finger to his soul, and there left its print.

The light came early on a cloudless day seven weeks before the solstice, three weeks on from the nightmare of Abbot John's visit to Motherwell; and when he heard the ringing of the bell for the office of the dawn, John was conscious that something further had shifted in his soul. He had prepared carefully what he wanted to say to his community in Chapter today, and he had a sense of the wounds in his soul beginning to granulate. All was not well, but his healing had moved along in the passing of time since his equilibrium had been so comprehensively shattered. And he had slept soundly, which made all the difference.

Father Gilbert read the chapter for that day, a beautiful May morning with the sound of birdsong carrying through the chapter house door that stood open to let in the fresh air and the joy of the sunshine. The chapter for the day was part of Benedict's discourse on the kind of man the abbot should be, and this section admonished the abbot to have no personal preferences among the brothers and not to elevate any above the others except as a man's own merit made appropriate.

Abbot John spoke to them then.

"Brothers, forgive me if you'd been hoping for some words of wisdom about this morning's chapter on the importance of your abbot not having favorites. I have no favorites; you all irritate me unbearably at one time or another, as I do you. Um . . . that *was* a joke, though I see from your faces that some of you didn't realize that. Sorry . . . that means I must look more irritable than I meant to, for much of the time.

"Anyway, it's Ascension Day next week, and that's what I wanted to talk to you about. I'm begging your indulgence now; please bear with me, for I want to make you listen to something I need to hear myself, something I'm trying to understand and trying to believe, but I haven't quite got there yet.

"What's been snagging at my soul in recent days is the thing Jesus said to Mary Magdalene in the story of Easter morning that we listened to a few weeks ago. He comes to her at this moment in which she thinks she's lost everything, because she's lost him. Her life has gone gray, and all its meaning is snuffed out. In the hour before dawn when everything is still hopelessly dark, she can't see him—can't recognize him, I mean—and she begs him to tell her where they have laid her Lord, so she can go and weep over the corpse of what used to be. But then Christ says her name, and suddenly she sees the living reality of him in her new situation. Naturally, in astonishment and delight she reaches out to embrace him. But he says, '*Noli me tangere*—don't touch me; for I have not yet ascended to the Father.' I have never understood these strange words, but I think I have found a glimpse into them in recent days.

"I don't need to tell you of my sorrow and anguish in this recent time—my mother murdered and my sister raped and left for dead. It's been just dreadful. It has tortured me beyond bearing to contemplate the thought of it. At the center of the horror, the thing that really crucified me was knowing that if I had been there and not here, I might have prevented it. I am used to the idea of a vocation being costly, but not to contemplating just how costly it could be for my family.

"In the middle of all this, I've felt entombed. Like a bird battering and bruising itself against the bars of its cage, my spirit has battered against the confines of earthly being, bruised by the appalling, inescapable realities of the things that happened, especially to my sister, who has been damaged—I think, irreparably.

"Crucified, then entombed—but there came a time to come back into the hurting, stabbing light of day, to try to be something better and more workable than simply out of my mind with horror, tormented by the nightmare my family went through.

"Now this is the thing I wanted to talk to you about. I have found, in this strange time, that I cannot bear to be touched. My own humanity has become unbearable to me. I have felt that if anyone touches me I will break completely, beyond what I feel I can endure. I thank you so much for having respected that. Nobody has tried to enfold me in an embrace to console me or put an arm round my shoulders or any of that. You have given me the *noli me tangere* space I've needed, emerging from the death of what reality used to be for me.

"But I am noticing that Christ said to Mary not just, 'Don't touch me,' but, 'Don't touch me; for I am not yet ascended to the Father,' which implies imminent change about to take place. Now then, here is my hope. Crucifixion, yes; emerging from the tomb into the painful light, yes; *noli me tangere*, yes; but what came next is that Christ *did* ascend to the Father, and when that happened, people all over the place were put into touch with him, accessing the transformative power of his life.

"My brothers, please don't think I am saying, 'Look at me, I am exactly like Christ'; for I *am not*! I am painfully, miserably conscious of how childishly self-centered my response has been to the impact of this horror and grief. All I mean is, in looking forward to the story of the Ascension, I have glimpsed hope. What I have been through felt like the tearing agony of crucifixion; before God, it did! I am not exaggerating. The only respite from it was when I fell into such darkness of despair it was like being sealed in a tomb. The strange imperative of seeming unable to bear the touch of any human being has felt like living in a kind of molten state, like a butterfly losing the integrity of its being in the pupation time of the chrysalis: to be touched, pried open, would bring complete disintegration. Again my brothers, I thank you for honoring that.

"But something in me sees—and loses sight of and then sees again and then loses again—a vision that where I am now, *noli me tangere*, is not the final word. This is but the hour before the dawn. The time of healing will come, and when it does, my spirit will find its way up to God's light and grace, will be enabled to rise above what has happened, will be empowered to grow into something new.

"What I was is dead and buried; what I am is in a half-formed, dissolved condition that barely holds together from day to day. I feel unrecognizable even to those who knew me the best. But I know that when I have grown into the new, when I have managed to crawl into the lap of God, I will be able to bear human touch again. You will be able to touch me because I shall be held fast in the heart of the Father.

"I feel the need to apologize to you, for I am not there yet. At the moment I am only half-formed—disintegrated, destroyed, pupated. Please bear with me and continue to pray for me— that in due course my spirit will rise out of this. Ascension Day drawing near has given me new hope—that there is a way up out of this, that one day my life will begin again—not as a reversion to what it used to be, but as a resurrection."

John spoke these words into a profound, receptive silence unsullied by restlessness. The community was gathered in focus and intent. They cared about him; they wanted his healing; they had prayed for him. He felt humbled by this unspoken strength that upheld him. When he stopped speaking, he had a sense of something being cleansed in him, an easing of pain allowing a possibility of peace. He could feel his way to the source of this change; it was because they had heard him, because they saw what life had done to him, and they held him gently, without questioning or reproof. They were giving him time to find his feet again, trusting him to come through into the light where they waited and held on for him. John bowed his head, grateful.

None of this meant that everything was instantly better; sorrow is not like that. Still John lay awake in bed most nights, sleep eluding him. Still he found he needed solitude and quietness. But he felt able to pick up the work that needed his attention. Again he felt humbled by his brothers' support on every side. Brother Ambrose or Father William would come to his lodging with bills to sign, and the matter was dealt with merely by writing his name and adding his seal. The precentor and sacristan managed the liturgical rhythm of monastic life without his input, and Father Theodore kept the novices safely under his own wing with no need for consultation with their abbot. Brother Michael oversaw the infirmary and Brother Cormac the kitchen. The gardens, the farm, the pottery, the guest house, and the school continued to run smoothly because they were well-managed. Father Chad was happy to intercept most of their guests. His brothers shielded him from involvement beyond what was strictly necessary. And gradually he was coming to himself again, getting the feel and the life of the place back into his hands as quickly as he could.

He had no way to tell his community how grateful he felt; he just hoped they felt it, as he felt the solid bulwark of their love and prayer. He did his best for them and for God, as they were also doing their best, but he could not evade the knowledge that something remained numbed and shuttered at the core of himself. He was still frozen in the space of *noli me tangere*.

He wondered if he would ever again, without any effort in the doing of it, reach out to touch with healing hands, put out his hand without stopping to think, to ascertain what the matter was and what he could do to help. He did not see what more he or anyone could do to thaw out the numbness that had taken hold of his heart.

Dutifully, every day, he had prayed for his sister and held her protectively in the light of God's love. He trusted that one day, by some means, she could be healed.

On that eve of the feast of the Ascension, Abbot John looked the picture of self-possession and composure as he sat at his capacious table spread with neat heaps of bills from the checker brought for the endorsement of his seal. Cautiously, and with a certain degree of amazement, he acknowledged to himself that he actually felt quite cheerful and no longer overwhelmed. He accorded himself a measure of approval. It had been, after all, only a month since the appalling news had been brought to him. He had struggled through to functionality with the best speed he could muster.

"Father John."

John looked up from the heap of documents on his table to see William standing there. It came into his mind that when anybody else looked at him, he felt merely held in that person's line of vision. When William looked at him, he felt as though those eyes were somehow penetrating the inmost recesses of his being. It occurred to him that William must have been a very good superior, if only he hadn't been such a thoroughly bad one.

"Yes?" he said.

"The door is wide open, else I should have knocked. Is it too late to ask if I may come in?"

"It would appear so. I will warn you, though, if you have brought me any more of your difficult contracts and deeds to look over, I shall fall irrecoverably into a dementia only to escape them."

William nodded thoughtfully. "You will have to tell me it has happened; else how shall I know? But look—am I disturbing you?"

"As you see. I have this pesky cellarer's assistant who lets nothing by him, not the smallest footling thing, and is making me examine *everything* because he has some shady ambition to drag us out of our Gospel simplicity into well-being and prosperity. I'm minded to get rid of him, but he won't go away. What is it?"

"Well, I have something on my conscience."

"On your *what?* Heaven bless us, this is new!"

Abbot John pushed his chair back from the table. Somewhat to his surprise, he found it moved silently. Looking down at the feet of it he saw that someone—presumably Tom—had stuck a little pad of felted wool under each foot. John wondered if every time he had pushed his chair back, it had grated on Brother Tom's nerves as well as on the stone flags of the floor. Tom had never said anything.

"Come in then, thou rogue; sit thee down. What's the thorn that has discovered thy conscience?"

William followed his abbot across to the two chairs near the hearth. Tom had laid the fire but this May morning had left it unlit. The men sat down together beside where the fire would have been.

"Since you're sitting here, and for once not prattling incontinently about some incomprehensible scheme of your own to make me sleep uneasy as you consolidate our wealth, there's something I've been intending to raise with you too, when the moment presented."

"Go on then," William responded. "You're my abbot. You first. 'Tis fitting."

From time to time when John found his thoughts focusing on William, he marveled at how valuable he had become to their community and gave silent thanks that they had not in lack of faith and in simple ignorance thrown this strange jewel away. During these awful weeks of struggle, John was vaguely aware that William had never been far from his side; quietly watching, working tirelessly to see that the day-to-day running of the abbey ran smoothly, that their investments and purchases were sound and their rents paid on time. Nobody tried to cheat William; it wasn't worth it, in all kinds of ways. Abbot John understood the cellarer's work well enough to know that this obedience fulfilled faithfully and intelligently made all the difference in the world to the abbot's work. He knew that, through all the nightmare, William had seen to it that the socket into which his daily life fitted was protective and secure. John understood too that in his detached and undemonstrative way, this shrewd and calculating soul loved him, but without burdening him with the usual human demands made by those who love—to be first, to be special, to be beheld and understood. Content to watch over him quietly, William kept his distance, but there was something about having him there that made John feel safe. He felt that in this man he had a friend who would notice and observe all his weaknesses, everything he felt ashamed of and wished he had not done, with perfect equanimity, simply seeing it was so. And he thought that in this if in nothing else, he saw something Christlike in William— acceptance of John's humanity, just as it was. Neither in awe of John's status nor afraid of his anguish, William's acceptance felt restful and even healing.

At this moment he was waiting imperturbably for his abbot to speak.

"It was only I wanted to say thank you," said John, "for everything you are doing here, which is quite literally worth its weight in gold, as you surely know. But also for all that you said to me the day we met with Madeleine. I've had occasion, many times in the course of more sleepless nights than I care to remember, to cling quite desperately to what you said to me then. It might be overconfident to say it's pulled me through, but I know it stopped me from going insane over it all."

William inclined his head slightly in acknowledgment of this. Under the composure of his features, a smile of appreciation faintly gleamed. "If I have helped, I am most glad," he replied, "for I believe I owe you everything."

It was rare for him to step out from behind the habitual irony of his persona, and John looked at him, intrigued. He had discovered that the gentle insults of affection suited William better than the claustrophobia of emotion. Hardly ever did he speak his heart in simple terms, and when he did, he was not comfortable staying long in that open intimacy. So John moved on.

"But what did you have on your 'conscience,' as I think you called it?"

"Well . . . Father . . . "

John frowned, puzzled and intrigued. In the first place William did not often address him as Father. "My lord abbot," he said more often, with a certain sardonic flourish, a hint of exaggerated formality, or often he avoided any form of address at all. The simplicity and intimacy of "Father" did not sit comfortably with him. Evidently whatever he had come to discuss, he was in earnest about it—and did not find it easy to say.

"Just a minute," said John; he got up from his chair, crossed the room, and closed the door to the cloister. The door to the abbey court, where villagers and visitors from afar most often entered his lodge, remained shut at all times except for specific admittance. But the cloister door stood open much of the time. John liked to be accessible to his brothers in community.

"What is it?" he asked as he took his seat again. "What's amiss?"

"I don't know that I can ask this. It seems a lot to ask."

"Out with it, man! What?"

"Well, Father, when you passed through Chesterfield, you said, on your return home to take up the reins of the abbacy here, you came across one of us from St. Dunstan's. You said you found him destitute."

John nodded. "I did. And left him as I found him, for which I have felt much ashamed. For a while my mind turned to him over and again, wondering what might have become of him; but of late there seems to have been little of me left over to contemplate any sorrows but my own. And when I say it, I am ashamed of that too."

William nodded. "Aye, likewise. You spoke to me of him when first I came here, but my own concerns pushed his away to the edge of my thoughts, and I'm sorry for it. But my intention wasn't to make you ashamed nor to wallow in my own shame either. I have opportunity to do that any day of the week."

The admission, spoken with dry humor, was, John judged, nonetheless sincere. William fascinated him. Sometimes he appeared hard, even ruthless; then he would say something like this that opened a narrow window offering a surprising glimpse into an unexpected interior. He was not without sensitivity or morality, whatever shell of indifference he chose for his shelter.

"I wondered," said William then, humbly and directly, "if we might go and look for him. It has plagued my conscience dreadfully. I feel safe here, but I was not safe out there, and nor will he be. How can I lift no finger to help him nor inquire what has become of him? How can I help myself to the peace and order of this house, knowing that I have left him to the mercy of the street? It has come to me more and more strongly that I should go and find him—nay, if I'm honest, that I should have gone long before this. But . . . well, the truth is, I am afraid to go.

"I know you have hardly had the chance to give your new position the attention it deserves. I know I have taken up inordinate quantities of your time and attention already. I know you have been through so much, it is an impertinence to ask you anything. I realize you must have matters awaiting your perusal and response stacked up to the rafters almost. I see full well that I have no right to ask. But though from our point of view it is an unwelcome extra intrusion into what has already been chaotic enough, I am asking myself if from his point of view he may have reached despair or fallen sick . . . or the Lord alone knows what may have befallen him.

"I think I must go and see if I can't find him, but I am afraid to go alone, for they do not love me in Chesterfield, nor anywhere else. And besides, you know where we might look for him."

"So when you say, 'Can we go and look for him?' you are meaning, 'Can we go right now?'"

William did not reply. He looked at his abbot. As John's eyes met the curious, shifting surface of William's gaze, like all places stony and wild, like all dangerous seas under a bleak sky, he found it odd that he had come to like him so much, and odder still to read in those aloof, feral eyes that William trusted him.

"Are you satisfied that Brother Ambrose—or 'Saint Ambrose' as I believe the brothers are calling him since he got his new assistant—can cope without your help?"

William nodded.

"Everything is in beautiful order, my lord abbot. Some promising investments are made—I am just waiting for word of a ship coming in to harbor, and I don't expect that quite yet. The Lady Day rents are all *finally* in—after a certain degree of necessary persecution. Everything else is sorted and folded and squared off and nailed down. If Saint Ambrose can't cope with things as they are, you need to get a new cellarer."

"Well, I think I have a new cellarer, in all but name, and you are doing a grand job, which I appreciate more than I can tell you. So we'll go together then?"

A gleam of gratitude illumined William's eyes.

"One thing, if I am to go with you, I ask in return."

William raised one eyebrow in silent inquiry.

"Tell me, William de Bulmer, what makes a good abbot in your estimation?"

Amusement flickered then. "I am surprised you ask that of me. Nobody here, so far as I knew, felt moved to link the word *good* with anything I ever did, let alone the kind of prior I made at St. Dunstan's!"

"Maybe. Even so?"

"Well, I can tell you readily enough, for it's a very simple thing. What makes a good abbot is anticipation. When times are hard, you have to have faith and vision for your community. When times are good, you have to be prudent and frugal and recognize that every pendulum swings. You have not only to see what your men need to be content now, but what they will need as times change, as they move on—as they grow more sophisticated or educated or complacent or weary or just old. You have to stay ahead of them. You have to know what they will think, what they will do, and what they are likely to say.

"It's the same thing as makes a good mother for a family— when the children are hungry, she has the pot already bubbling; when they are tired, her feet are already on the path home from the market; when the baby starts to toddle and get adventurous, she has already mended the hole the fox made in the fence."

John listened to this, intrigued. "I'd not have had you down as a man who gave much thought to being a good mother!"

William's face twisted in the dry irony of something that wasn't really a smile. "I do not give it much thought. But I know what a bad mother is."

John regarded him thoughtfully. "I see," he said. William shifted, uneasy, lest that should be true.

"Then, can we go?"

"It seems a good time," John affirmed. "All is in hand here, and circumstances have kept me from becoming engrossed in matters I could not easily leave. Thanks in the main to your good work, all things temporal are well tended. As to matters spiritual, I judge myself still in a condition to be of very little use for wise counsel. This thing should have been dealt with before in any case; so yes, let's go! Will you see to our mounts and some food for the journey? Chesterfield is three days' ride from here at best. I'll look for Father Chad and arrange the rest; we can start in the morning, straight after we've said the morrow Mass. Had you stopping places along the way already in mind?"

William hesitated. "I thought . . . " His eyes flickered, and he looked away for a moment, unwilling to meet his abbot's gaze. John wondered why.

"I thought we might save some money; this dry spell looks set to continue, and the nights are warm for May. Let's see how we get on rolled in a blanket in the hedgerow or borrow a bed in a barn somewhere."

John shrugged, as happy with this plan as any. Inns and hostels usually smelt rank and had flea infestations. An open-air bed had much to commend it. He accepted the suggestion on face value. Not until much later when he sat in quiet meditation before Vespers did the source of William's disquiet dawn on him. It was because he was afraid. He could not face the reception that might await him at the various religious houses that lay on their path to Chesterfield.

CHAPTER
FOUR

I found him in an alley near the market; it was just beside a bakehouse. I remember because I went to get us some bread. I was almost out of money, but I thought we could share a loaf."

The two men picked their way along the crowded streets of the busy town, John retracing his steps with increasing confidence. Having run back and forth to provide food and water for the destitute man on the first time of visiting the place, he remembered the location of St. Mary's Gate and the alleyway beside the baker's shop without too much trouble.

"There he is! In the exact same place where I left him! That's too good to be true! Look, William, we've found him!"

The man he had seen had a considerable beard and his tonsure had a covering of dark hair by now, but John recognized him from across the street, even still wearing the same habit he had seen him in before. His face was turned toward them, but he gave no sign of recognition.

Then in the next moment John's exultation withered into shriveling horror as, crossing the street together, William said quietly, "Look again. It seems to me that someone else has found him first."

As they traversed the thoroughfare and came to the mouth of the alley, hearing passing feet pause before him, the crouching beggar became very still and attentive—and wary. Standing in front of him, William and John found the impression formed as they crossed the road confirmed. They were looking down on the swollen, damaged eye sockets of a blinded man.

"Father Oswald," said William, "it's me."

The man was galvanized into response by these words. He did not say anything, which seemed odd to John, nor did he smile; but he reached out filthy hands in sleeves thick with blood and dirt and stuck food scraps and turned his face eagerly toward William's voice.

John glanced at William, taken aback that he did not come down to his brother's level, did not touch him or take his hand to make connection with the poor man in his blindness. He saw that William was looking very closely at the mutilated man, frowning as he scrutinized his face. Oswald's lips were swollen and crusty, and blood had dried in clots and rivulets into his beard. Sores had been created at the corners of his mouth by a constant trickle of saliva that Oswald periodically raised his hand to wipe away.

Slowly William squatted down in front of him. "Speak to me," he said softly. And then John understood.

Oswald spoke, but he produced no human speech—only a guttural moaning that formed no words.

"Oh holy Jesus! Oh sweet mother of God! What have they done to him?" gasped John as he bent over the man. Oswald reacted sharply to his voice, which he clearly recognized at once. He had not forgotten John. He reached out his hands toward them, groping to make contact.

"Put out his eyes and cut out his tongue, as I think you can see," said William. "And God only knows what else we shall discover in due course."

As William spoke, John knelt down before the crouching man and let the questing hands find him. Horror jolted through him in waves that left him cold and trembling. The bright sunshine of the day seemed only pitiless now. "Oh, why? Why did I not come back? How could I have left him? Why ever did I not come back?"

As he allowed the man to cling to him, moaning out his incomprehensible words, his face searching blindly toward John, his hands clutching at him desperately, tears streamed down John's face.

"Oh, *why* did I not come back?"

"You did come back," said William. "You are here."

Blowing out his breath in an effort to regain calm, John brushed his tears away.

The maimed beggar continued to cling to him, gripping the folds of John's cloak tightly, pouring out words that neither man could understand.

"Just a minute. Steady, my brother; it's all right; we shall not leave you. Wait while I sort myself out."

John blew his nose and wiped his tears away, his hands still trembling. Then he pushed his handkerchief back into his pocket, and William watched the remorse and distress receding to be dealt with later as John brought his skills and experience to the situation.

"Let's have a look at you." John's voice, kind and sane, disciplined into composure again, spoke reassurance.

"Open your mouth," he said gently. "Let me see. Well, that has healed fairly clean at least. Hold still now, very still. I want to look at your eyes. I will not hurt you, but you must keep still. These are sore and swollen, and that's pus oozing there. You've got quite a bit of dirt in the sockets I think, my brother. How could you not, out on the street like this? They need cleaning and soothing. I think you will need bandages, maybe eye patches. I have never cared for an eye socket before; we will have to learn together. But we can take care of you and make you comfortable.

"This is strange, William. How has he survived? Has someone helped him? The blood loss when someone's tongue is cut out is phenomenal. The shock of losing both eyes and tongue could result in death by itself."

"His mouth looks burned to me. I think they did something to stem the bleeding. Can you see? Probably not in this alley; it's not the best place for light. Maybe he was just lucky, if that's the right word."

"But why would anyone do this? Is it simply the viciousness of human nature—because he was vulnerable here on the street?"

"No." William shook his head. "He will have been recognized. Oswald was my almoner. We were not known for giving freely. There will have been many he turned away." He straightened up and stood watching as John took Oswald's hands in his left hand, keeping that gentle contact as he continued to look carefully at Oswald's eyes and mouth, his right hand touching lightly to help him feel and see what had happened as he explored and examined. Oswald was quiet now, his face turned toward John in mute attention.

"Well, he was no angel," William observed drily, watching, "but he didn't deserve this."

"We have to get this poor soul to shelter," said John firmly. He turned to look up at William. "Where is the nearest Benedictine house from here?" He frowned. "What? William, how do you make your eyes kind of flicker like that when you don't like what's said to you?" A look of amusement passed through William's face, and John could never figure out how he did that either: how he could smile but not smile. "Well?" he pushed him.

"There is a house ten miles north of here," William replied. "It lies barely a half mile out of our journey home. St. Olave's at Holmehurst."

"Perfect. Let's go there then. What's the matter?"

William moved his hand in a vague, irritable gesture of dismissal. "'Tis only a matter of a few months since their abbot denied me shelter in the roundest possible terms. Threatened to set his dogs on me if ever I darkened his door again."

John stood up. "Did he so! Who is their abbot?"

"Robert Chesham."

"Why is he keeping dogs?"

William shrugged. "He's your modern Benedictine. Very sophisticated—or thinks he is. Rides to hounds and likes to go hawking with his friends in the aristocracy. Sees Nursia as very rustic and a far cry from fourteenth-century Chesterfield. He's not into the simple living your Columba held so dear."

"Very elegant. Well, I don't care if he keeps parrots and monkeys so long as he'll have us too. Anyway, you're a Benedictine now, so he doesn't have to like you, but he'll have to take you in. And Oswald will be a Benedictine before the fortnight's out. In the meantime he could be anything, so no need to take offense at him. We'll set out for Holmehurst directly. Don't look so skeptical; it'll be all right."

William went back for their horses, and John noticed that even crossing the street he looked as cautious and wary as a fox. When he returned, John helped Oswald to his feet. "He'd better ride up behind you; that's a better mount than my swaybacked old mare. Not that there's much of either one of you, but even so."

The evening sun lay warm on the pale stone of the gatehouse as they rode up to the entrance of St. Olave's. As they came to a halt, William and John looked at each other.

"Well, I'm not going to knock. I tell you, it's barely four months since they told me to get out of here and never come back, and my guess is they told Oswald the same. It's you who will have to ask."

Oswald commented on this. Neither of them understood him, but he seemed to be affirming William's remarks.

"Hold the reins for me then, and I'll see what they will do for us."

John knocked at the postern door in the great gates, which were shut, and at once their porter came out to him, smiling a welcome.

"God give you good day, Brother Porter," said John

courteously. "I am seeking lodging for a night for myself and my brothers. I am Abbot John Hazell of St. Alcuin's Abbey, north of York. My friends are also brothers of that house."

"Come in; you are right welcome, friend!" beamed the porter, grasping John's arm in hospitable goodwill. "My name is Brother Justin. Have you traveled far?"

"We are returning from Chesterfield," began John, but Brother Justin was no longer listening. His eyes had fallen upon William and whoever was seated behind him on his gray palfrey. He froze completely, staring at William, whose gaze, eyebrows lifted in sardonic inquiry, met his steadily.

The porter whirled about, asking John bluntly, "You have taken William de Bulmer into your house? You took him in?"

All of John's life had been bedded in a context of harmonious relationships. His childhood home had been happy, and his friendships with the other village lads had been cordial, and his work as infirmarian at St. Alcuin's brought him gratitude as well as fulfillment. As William and Oswald sat on the horse waiting for him to manage the porter's appalled response, he suddenly had a glimpse into the vulnerability of human existence: how much we depend upon the kindness and goodwill of others.

"He came to our house seeking shelter after the tragic fire at St. Dunstan's priory," said John evenly. "He was well known to us and had offered hospitality to our brothers in the past."

"Aye," replied the porter, "we know! Our prior was there as witness to that hospitality; it has not been forgotten."

John looked at the ground for a moment, embarrassed by the candid hostility and distressed for William and Oswald. He raised his eyes again to meet the porter's expression of frank indignation. "Well," he said softly, "he was grateful that we made space for him, and he is proving to be a wonderful asset to our community—both loving and remarkably able. We appreciate him. What's past is past; ours is to forgive, if I've read the Gospel right. Yours too, Brother Porter: same Gospel."

Nobody who lacks character and determination is ever elected abbot. Brother Justin noted the steel in John's gaze as it held his, though John's stance remained relaxed and friendly.

"May we come in?" Something in the way John said it communicated an expectation rather than a plea, but the porter remained reluctant.

"Who else is it you've got up there then?" he asked suspiciously. And at that John saw red.

"Since you ask," he replied, and his tone was different now—distinctly cold and clipped, "it is another brother of St. Dunstan's. Another who met your frigid welcome before. We came back to search for him, knowing him to have been left destitute. We found him on the street, with his eyes put out and his tongue cut off, left to the mercy of cruel and violent men because his Christian brothers found themselves too pure and too nice to bear his company. That's a sin of commission resting on a sin of omission by my calculation, and I am not favorably impressed. Seems to me it is a virtue these men can bear *your* company, never mind what you may think of them! At least you sleep safe at night and can swallow your food and see the light of day. Now will you let us in, or am I asking you to fetch your superior out here to speak with me?"

William slipped down from the horse and stepped quietly to his side. "Leave it, Father," he murmured. "If I am not welcome, I think I can make my own way home. If only they will take you in with Oswald, so he can be made comfortable for this night at least."

John didn't even look at him. "You will *not* ride home alone!" he answered shortly. "We can care for one mutilated man in our infirmary, but I see no point in adding a second."

"Come in, come in—let me open the way!" Flustered, Brother Justin averted his eyes and turned away, hurrying back in through the postern door to unlatch the big gate. "You can tie up your horses here," he said hastily as they came through; he evidently intended them to pass no farther. "Make yourselves comfortable yonder in the lodge. I think I'd better tell Abbot Robert you are here. I'll not keep you long."

In silence John hitched his old mare to the iron ring in the wall. "I hope she fouls his entranceway good and proper!" he muttered as William led his palfrey to the adjacent tethering ring. William shook his head, amusement gleaming in his face. "It's all right. I understand. I had it coming, and I have to live with it."

John laughed shortly. "Yea, verily, evil swine that you are!" he mocked him gently. "But I need you at my side, for you've kept me together in the bitter valley of these last weeks. I don't know what I should have done without you."

Again came the subliminal luminescence that did William most of the time for a smile. "I don't doubt you would have coped. You're sturdy-made. Look out, here comes Abbot Robert, just as promised! I'll get Oswald down: that'll give them food for thought. Come on down, my brother: look pitiful and earn us some supper and a night's lodging. If they give our abbot any grief, *you* talk to 'em!"

Oswald smiled, which in his present condition was an alarming sight in itself. He dismounted unaided and put out his hand to find William, who said to him, "I'm here" and let Oswald find his own way to his side.

Abbot Robert arrived at the entrance arch where they stood. A burly man in his midfifties, his face bore the story of the years in hard lines and clever eyes. He looked like a man who would stand no nonsense, and he threw one chilly glance at William before addressing his attention to John. "Father John, welcome! We have not met before. Brother Justin here tells me you need one night's lodging." He spoke pleasantly, but he emphasized *one*. John was a peaceable man, but he had fire about him too, and he did not take kindly to this.

"Aye; one, for our necessity," he said, "and then we shall be glad to go."

Abbot Robert's eyelids flickered slightly as he took in this reply.

"Father, may I speak?" murmured William submissively in his abbot's ear; and thinking of his usual manner of conducting himself, John wondered if there was no end to his tactical wiliness. "Certainly," he affirmed.

"Father Robert . . . " William's voice conveyed nothing of either its habitual mockery or the dangerous softness it could sometimes employ; neither did it allow Abbot Robert to see the vulnerability he exposed to John and his brothers at St. Alcuin's. He spoke with the humble and seemingly guileless simplicity of an artful child who knows how to get his own way. "I have by God's grace been given a new beginning with the good brothers of St. Alcuin's, who are true Christians indeed and a credit to their Lord, for they have taken me in. By their kindness I have been shown a better way. By their example I have seen what a monk may be. So you need fear no bad influence from me if I stay in your house this one night. I know you do not think the same as the brothers of St. Alcuin's; but I hope you will find in your heart the kindness to let us stay."

John saw in that moment—as he watched Abbot Robert looking closely at William's submissive innocence, trying to work out if he had just been breathtakingly insulted or not—why so many people hated William so much.

And then Abbot Robert started violently as Oswald added his own plea to the mix.

"Glory, what kind of a circus are we?" said John to William as twenty minutes later they made their way from the stables into the guest house, where they had been offered supper before they bedded down for the night. Father Robert had invited John to sup in the abbot's lodging, but John took exception to this pointed exclusion of his brothers and sweetly explained that his skills as an infirmarian might be called upon to help Oswald manage his food. Father Robert seemed content not to push this by asking how Oswald had been managing until now without John's help, graciously bowing his farewell to them as he withdrew.

The guest master showed them their chambers, where they stowed their baggage. John, as their abbot, had been given a room of his own; William and Oswald were given a room to share.

"Father Oswald, of your courtesy," said John gently, "will you mind sleeping alone and allowing William to room in with me?" He saw the relief on William's face as he said this, adding, "He is assisting our cellarer at home, and we have a number of things outstanding to discuss that are tedious to anyone else and may intrude on your rest as we talk. Will that arrangement please you?"

Oswald had been a monk for twenty-four years, and his prior had been William de Bulmer. He knew better than to say it didn't suit him, whatever his private thoughts might have been, and accepted the arrangement with good grace, though somewhere deep inside he knew he would be frightened when they left him alone.

"Right!" said John briskly as he and William dumped their bags on their beds. "I'm going down to the infirmary to beg a clean habit and a razor. I'll ask the guest master what their bathing arrangements are, and we'll get you clean and present-able before we sit down to eat. I shan't be long."

William guided Oswald into his chamber. "Just a min-ute—don't sit down yet," he said. He went to his own room and fetched the cloak he had deposited there, spreading it on the clean pale wool of Oswald's blankets to save them from the dried blood and food and the filth of the street that mired Oswald's garments from neck to hem. "You can sit down now— just one step directly behind you," he said. Oswald, looking ill at ease, sat on the bed. William sat beside him.

"Your tongue, your eyes—is that all?" he asked him crisply, and Oswald shook his head. The grim cruelty of what human beings will stoop to moved like a shadow through William's face. He said soberly, "Abbot John has been St. Alcuin's infirmarian these many years. He will see to what must be done to make the best of this. You could not be in a safer pair of hands."

Oswald nodded. He spoke, but William could not understand him. He said it again. "Thank you?" said William, and Oswald nodded. "For?" Oswald nodded. "Say the rest again." Oswald said it twice. "Coming back for you?" Oswald nodded.

Because his brother could not see, William did nothing to disguise the bleakness of this situation from showing in his face. But he said, "You are most welcome. I am only sorry that I did not come sooner; I had some struggles of my own."

As they waited together, William covered the silence that lay between them with quiet talk of St. Alcuin's Abbey, describing to Oswald the contours of the land and the extent of the buildings, telling him about its traditions of music and style of pottery, the size of the farm and the focus of its husbandry, the location in relation to the villages and towns nearby. As the anodyne flow of his words continued, he watched Oswald begin to relax, his mind led out of the fear of violence and hatred and danger into the consideration of the simple realities of everyday life—buildings and communities, routines and the comfortable patterns of tradition.

Then John stood in the doorway, an old habit from the infirmary in his arms. "We can take you to wash, Father Oswald, and I will shave your head and beard. Come to that, William, you look much like a vagrant yourself—a little soap and water would do you no harm."

John and Oswald rejoined William in time for supper. "It is as you thought," John said quietly to William, "they were not satisfied with what they did to his face. Whatever the countenance of pity looks like, it is not human."

William shrugged. "Some and some," he said and added, "Yes, he told me."

The guest master brought them bread and cheese, apples and ale, with a pat of freshly made butter still beaded with moisture in an earthenware dish.

Oswald looked like a monk again, his beard shaved and his hair trimmed and tonsured, dressed in St. Olave's clean habit.

John had also begged a large cloth from the infirmarian. He said gently to Father Oswald as he took his place at the table, "Father, will you let me provide you with a napkin to keep your habit clean? My guess is, supper has become something of an adventure to you now." Oswald laughed, from which sight William silently looked away, and John spread the cloth carefully, tying the ends of it at the back of Oswald's neck. When he had done, he rested his hands in reassurance on Oswald's shoulders and said, "I am here beside you if you find yourself in need of any help."

Oswald replied. John and William looked at each other blankly. "Say that again," said William, and Oswald did. "Oh, right! You can manage!" John's face cleared. "Yes, I expect you can. Here's bread, brother, and cheese and butter. I'll put some here on your plate; butter on the edge. There's ale too. Would you like some milk to dip your bread? I'll ask our guest master. There are apples, but those will not work for you I think?"

Oswald shook his head, saying "no apples," which the shake of his head and the *p* in *apples* helped them recognize. He nodded his head then, affirming *milk*, and stroking his left finger with his right hand in the sign for milk from the *Monasteriales Indicia*, the sign language of the monastic hours of silence. John requested some from the guest master who was happy to oblige.

Oswald next spoke to John again, but however often he repeated it, neither man could understand. He reached out his hand, groping for John, whose hand found his. "You—" Oswald managed to make himself understood at last, and he traced the word *kind* in unsteady letters with his forefinger on the tabletop.

"You notice he doesn't extend the same compliment to me," said William drily, pulling them back from the territory of emotion into the verges of which they were straying.

As they ate together, the magnitude of what had been done to Oswald made itself obvious. William watched him, remembering his fastidious manners. The son of a merchant with aspirations to upward mobility in society, Oswald had been schooled in courtly graces until the end of his teens, when his father had lost three spice ships and most of his money, the large mansion in which they lived had to be sold, and it had been expedient for both his sons to discover in themselves the stirrings of religious vocation—quickly. At St. Dunstan's Priory Oswald was sometimes admired, sometimes mocked for his elegance and refinement. William watched as Oswald broke his bread and dipped it in the milk, dropping lumps that he groped for and carried to his mouth, dripping milk and wet shreds of bread. Of the food he got safely into his mouth, some fell out, and what remained he had to push back to his throat with his fingers. Some he swallowed successfully; some he had to hawk back up and start again because it went the wrong way. William took a little cheese, a little bread, then found himself suddenly not hungry anymore.

Abbot John ate his supper quietly and steadily, occasionally reaching out to guide Oswald's hand or put back on his plate bread he had inadvertently pushed off. The cheese and the apples were beyond Oswald's attempting. At the conclusion of their meal, the table around Oswald's bowl and plate was strewn with spilled food, and the cloth that wrapped him was drenched with milk and soggy bread. John removed the cloth, careful to keep any mess contained within it, and used it to wipe down the table, talking amiably as he did so of their journey home. By the time he'd finished, the chaos of Oswald's supper had vanished from view.

"Are we going to Compline?" John was not sure to what degree his companions would feel comfortable participating in the life of St. Olave's.

"For sure we are!" said William at once. "It'll be one more strike against us if we are too corrupt to bother to worship God!"

Oswald offered a comment with a conspiratorial nudge. After persevering with decoding his remark for quite some while, John and William grasped that what he had said was he would sing loudly. As they walked from the guest house across to the cloister buildings, John reflected that the refusal of St. Dunstan's survivors to take themselves seriously showed they had strength of character even if they had admittedly been lacking in virtue.

After Compline, the community went into silence, and the three travelers returned to their rooms in the guest house, making ready to retire for the night. John could see Oswald's distress and deep sense of misgiving as he prepared to leave him on his own. He could not even leave him a light to dispel the oppression of darkness. He contemplated changing the sleeping arrangement but suspected William might be dismayed to find himself rooming in with Oswald; and he himself felt so distressed and unsettled by this turn of events that he wanted some time to talk it through in privacy with William. He had taken a linen towel from the lavatorium, and he spread it on Oswald's pillow to soak up the frequent streams of saliva that dribbled from his mouth.

"Lie down," he said to him gently. "I'll stay with you for a little while. And we are only in the chamber next door. You would be able to find us, and we would hear you call. All will be well. These are good men here. Their welcome may have been frostier than it should have been, but you will sleep safe from harm. The worst they will do to us is leave us alone. Rest now, my brother. Say your prayers quietly until you fall asleep. Here, you can have my rosary." John stayed a while longer until the atmosphere changed and he saw Oswald begin to relax; then he bade him good night and left the room. He joined William in the adjacent chamber and closed the door.

Even so late in the evening, it was not quite dark at this time of year. The last light of day still filtered in through the small windows, but William had lit the candle, as much for hope and cheerfulness as to see.

John crossed the room in silence and sat on the edge of his bed without speaking, bending to take off his sandals. His face was grave and troubled as he climbed into bed. He sat with his back leaning against the wall that the head of his bed abutted, staring straight ahead, thinking.

William also said nothing, but he was waiting for John to speak, which eventually he did, words pouring out in a torrent of the distress he had succeeded in concealing from Oswald. "How could I have let this happen?" he berated himself bitterly. "I can't live with this, William. I can't bear it. My sister raped and battered, my mother murdered, and now this poor soul tortured and abused and left with his life ruined forever. Can't see. Can't speak. Can't eat properly. What do they think of when they do things like this to people? Another human being—all the joy of life snuffed out and exchanged for terror and death in the work of one short evening. Who can make an eye? Who can give the gift of sight? Who can understand or make a copy of the tongue—to talk, to taste, to feel, to swallow, to moisten the lips, to kiss? How dare they destroy what they did not give and cannot make? What cruel, savage ignorance! The delicate, beautiful, intricate integrity of God's creation, everything working together to make life joyous and sweet—aye, to make life *possible* at all—just thrown away. And am I not just as bad, just as much to blame? For I sat with him there in that alley in

Chesterfield, broke bread with him. I *found* him, and then I left him behind, threw him back, to this! How could I have done it? How could I have left him? Oh God, I cannot live with the guilt of this. I cannot bear it. And my mother. And my sister. It's too much, it's just too much. I cannot bear it." He sat trembling, unable to process the horror of all that had happened.

"Sshh! Listen a minute!" William's faint gleam of a smile shone for a moment, but he spoke soberly then. "Listen. Are you listening or just caught in a tangle of grief and guilt and shock?"

The haggard strain in John's face was accentuated by the light of the candle that burned on the table beside him as he looked at William. *You've aged about ten years in this last month*, William thought.

"I'm listening," said his abbot.

"Good. Because there's something and someone you've forgotten. Now listen to this. When I came to you before Easter, it was for exactly what we've seen today that I was afraid to be turned out. I've seen other men branded, gelded, mutilated—their hands cut off, their ears, their noses slit in two. I knew well what kind of business the pack would wish to do with me. We were a sinful house, Father; and worse than that, we were successful and rich. The world rubs along with sin easily enough—but success? The rich are hounded without mercy by a thousand hangers-on and must expect to pay out generously or be hated. We didn't pay. We had no mercy either. And we were hated, me especially.

"What think you? If you had not stood between me and Brother Thomas's old loyalties—between me and Father Chad's fears and Father Gilbert's misgivings—where do you think I should have been? Dangling and jerking from a tree branch dying at my own hand most likely—and that would have been the easy, gentle choice. Or I'd have been kicked to death or choking on my own blood as they sliced out *my* tongue, groping blind and in agony as they tore out *my* eyes despite my pleading and my screams, crawling to some corner in trembling shock after they cut off my sex organs. I knew very well what my fate would have been, and the evidence of it we've found crouched in the alley this evening. It would have been me begging on the street corner with the flies crawling into my eye sockets to lay their eggs. And who would have saved me but you? I heard Brother Thomas say he wished I'd been burnt to death; I believe he also expressed the opinion that someone should flay the skin off my back just as Christ was flayed. Nay, it's all right—it's all right; I understand. He's a passionate man, and we are friends now. But if you had stayed home with your mother, if you had stayed in Chesterfield with Oswald, who would have been there for me? You'd forgotten that, hadn't you? You hadn't thought of it like that. No, but I surely haven't forgotten. If you had delayed *one day* to care for Oswald on your way home or to find means to bring him with you, then when I arrived at St. Alcuin's you would not yet have arrived home. And do you think they would even have let me in past the porter's lodge if you had not been there? Well? You know as surely as I do, they would not. I give thanks every day that my life was given to me twice—once by the hand of God when I was born of my mother, and once by you. And you might take a break from beating yourself up over the things you missed and the things you got wrong to notice that sometimes you got it splendidly, mercifully right. Nobody can be everyplace at once and save everybody, but by God, Father John, I'm glad you were there for me!

"And what if you had—quite reasonably—found yourself too fully occupied to come with me in search of Oswald? What if you had contented yourself with giving me directions to know where to look? Do you think these good brothers would have taken us in without you? Did it escape you, the way they looked at me and the opinion they hold of me? There would have been nothing but a bed in the lee of a hedge or huddled in a church porch all the way home if you had not been with us—and what if I had been recognized on the way? Oh, my lord abbot, it's easy to make an inventory of the things you could have done and failed to do, but if you're bent on doing that, you must remember the times you were there and it made a difference."

Abbot John sat quietly, digesting these words. "Thank you," he said after a while. "Thank you, William. You always comfort me."

Mindful then of the Grand Silence, which should be broken only of necessity, they spoke no more. John blew out the candle, and they settled down under their blankets, but neither of them could sleep. An hour dragged by, and another. Wide-eyed, John stared into the darkness, remembering his sister's anger and coldness, seeing her face and hearing her words again: "No doubt it would have been different if you'd been there." He tried not to think of his mother but found himself wondering how quick it had been and whether she had been very afraid. And he relived the supper they had just shared, Oswald's painful, choking progress through a bowl of milky sops.

Haunted by memories, John tried to pray. He prayed for himself, for forgiveness and strength; and for Oswald, for courage and grace; for his sister and the community she lived in now, that she would find peace. He prayed for the repose of his mother's soul. And he prayed for William, who had been turning restlessly in his bed the entire time.

"What? What's troubling you?" Abbot John finally spoke into the midnight, addressing the edginess he could feel in his companion.

"Did I wake you? I'm sorry. I didn't mean to disturb you."

"I suspect you have always been more than a little disturbing to everyone you meet." William heard the smile in his abbot's reply. "But, no, you didn't wake me up. It's just I can feel that something is troubling you."

He listened to the sound of William turning in his bed, sighing, finally struggling into a sitting position, and sighing again.

"What?" John repeated.

"I can hardly say this. I feel so ashamed."

In the silence of the night John waited for him to speak, and finally William said, "The thing is . . . Oswald . . . my response is not like yours. I knew I had to go back and look for him, do what I could to find him. I knew I couldn't just help myself to safety and leave him behind, but . . . "

"Yes?" John prompted after some time went by.

"I don't want to take care of him," William mumbled. "He's going to be a confounded nuisance forever now, isn't he? Incessantly needy, trapped in his own body. It won't only be the appalling disabilities that have been imposed upon him; I mean, it isn't too hard I suppose to help someone get from place to place and make sure they have something to eat and someone to talk to . . . although . . . " Again William paused for a long time before admitting, "I don't want to do even that. It drives me wild having needy people tagging along with me. But the worst thing is, there's going to be an absolute tornado of grief and despair and tears and 'why me?' and religious doubt and all the rest of it unleashed once we get him to a place where he isn't just concentrating on surviving—isn't there? And all that makes me feel as if I'm drowning. I simply can't stand it. I mean, I wish he'd just died if we're going to have to live through all that. But people never can keep it contained, can they? They have to talk about it and weep about it and tell you how completely broken they are and all the rest of it."

He shifted restlessly. "I was his superior. I asked to go and find him. I'm responsible for bringing him back. So I guess that means I'll have to look after him and keep him company; listen to him and figure out the meaning of his weird moaning from day to day; take his arm and lead him every time he wants to go to the privy—and misses the hole—or it's time to go to chapel; sit with him and help him while he slobbers his food and pushes

it off the side of his dish, poking his fingers into it and trying
to find what he's got and where it is and trying to get it down
his gullet without choking to death. And what about the office?
D' you think he'll attempt to sing the psalms? Every time? Will
we have to put up with that forever? And what's this going to
mean about the community's attitude to me? They can barely
tolerate me as it is: I'm there because you fought tooth and
nail to keep me there. What will they think when we turn up
at home with Oswald in tow: 'Oh look, everybody; William's
brought his friend! Happy days!' *Sancta Maria!*"

He fell silent for a little while; then, by the faint moonlight
in the room, John saw his head turn toward his abbot. "And I
feel so dreadfully ashamed," William whispered, "that after all
you've done for me, I can't do better than this. It's disgraceful,
isn't it? I'm a disgraceful man, and I should probably never
have been a monk. I certainly never thought I had a vocation.
But here I am now, and what on earth am I going to do? I never
even liked the man. Irritating individual. I can't bear all this
intimate, personal stuff, and I just *can't stand it* when people
slobber their food. It makes me feel sick."

"Is that all?" asked his abbot after a further silence had
elapsed.

"Yes."

John considered what he had just heard.

"Are you . . . are you really disappointed in me?" William
asked. "Are you sitting here thinking how pitiless and cruel I
am?"

"No, not that. I love your honesty, which I think takes courage. I love it that you don't pretend to be the man you think
you should be. I'm not disappointed in you. When someone's life
goes badly wrong, starting with reality is helpful. When we add
pretense to personal tragedy, we just give ourselves two impos-
sibilities to struggle with. For what it's worth, you may feel
reassured to know, every time I try to approach in my own mind

the fact that very soon, once I've figured out how to clean out his eye sockets thoroughly, I'm going to have to suture his eyelids, it makes me go cold inside—makes me feel like running away."

"Stone the crows!" said William's appalled voice into the silence that followed John's words. "I should think it does!"

The two men contemplated this hideous prospect as they gazed into the dark.

"Will he be able to sit still enough to let you do it? I mean— you won't be able to leave gaps or anything, will you? Because once you've stitched them you won't be able to get in to clean them."

"That's correct. I mustn't get it wrong. I've never done it before, and it's going to hurt him. I have to keep telling myself, if it feels too much to face for me, what must it feel like for him? Still, whatever he or I think or feel, it's got to be done, so there's an end of it. I'll find out what to do and take it from there. But can I ask you about something else? In all you told me just now, you said in passing that you never had a vocation. So what are you doing in monastic life?"

William reached down and pulled his cloak up from the floor, wrapped it around his shoulders. The days were warm now, in May, but the hours of darkness drew in cold.

"I like power and wealth. I like silence and beautiful music. I like fine art and good craftsmanship. I like spacious buildings. I had no stomach to be a soldier and no money for an apprenticeship. I worked for my father—he was a merchant—but things got too bad at home. I craved peace. My family did not love me, nor did I love them. There was nothing lost in parting from them, but I had to live somewhere. And I find women tiresome. It seemed the obvious choice."

"So you had no sense of being drawn by Christ into this way—or desire to come closer to him?"

"Christ?" William turned the question over thoughtfully. "When you speak about Christ—or when Theodore does or

Francis—it is the same as when Columba spoke of Christ. To listen to you, anyone would think you meant somebody actually real—somebody you know, your master maybe or your friend."

"That's right," said John softly.

"Well, that isn't what most people mean."

The wide spaces of the night expanded around them. John had that odd feeling of limitlessness that comes in the deepest hours of the night—a time when anything might happen; a time when people die and truth is spoken, when animals lie down to give birth to their young. He listened to the silence and felt the spaces, felt his own soul expand into the spacious night. "What do most people mean by 'Christ'?" he asked.

William pondered this question. "Most people mean one of two things," he replied after some thought. "Either way it is an object, not a person. Either they see Christ as an important asset—like a tool or weapon or a game piece. If you can prove you have Christ on your side, you win the game. If you have Christ in your hand, your arsenal is superior to that of those who don't. Religious argument is about establishing that my argument has Christ in it, not yours—so that you have to capitulate and I win. Or else they see Christ as the object of a set of ideas. The concepts formulate around the second member of the Trinity and fix him into his place in the dogma of the church. The dogma is mandatory then—hence the Christ idea being useful as a tool or weapon: something to get your own way with. Not all people manipulate things that cynically, of course, though it can certainly be done; I've done it myself.

"But many believe faithfully all their lives without ever realizing that their faith is just the pursuit of self-interest ratified by being able to produce 'Christ' in substantiation of their own theory or objective. Whoever has Christ wins.

"But when *you* speak about Christ, in Chapter, it is as it was when Columba spoke of him. You are not trying to work an angle or push through your own advantage, and you don't care who wins. But you—I don't know—it's as though Christ were not just a matter of belief but somebody you know, someone you've personally met, I mean . . . and you love him."

"Yes. That's right," John replied. "That's how it is."

"How your religious faith is? You mean that faith for you is a personal thing, so real it's like actually knowing someone?"

"Yes," said John, then, "No!"

He sat up in his bed. "D' you know, if it had been daylight, I'm not sure I could have found it within myself to say this. It feels too personal. You are a master of the searching question! How you just put it—what did you say? That for me religious faith has a personal nature, almost like actually knowing someone? No—that's not it. Religious faith is something a man *has*, like an attribute of that man. In one man it's a thing of the heart, in another it's a thing of the head. It's a conviction, it's whatever you like to call it, but it's part of the man. But really knowing—meeting—finding Christ is not an attribute or a conviction. It doesn't arise from the seeker. Christ is really there. He *is* someone I know, someone I've personally met. And I do love him."

"This is like a mystical experience that you're describing?"

"Well . . . more for every day than that. I don't mean a caught-up-into-the-divine, glimpse-of-heaven type of thing. And it isn't 'like' anything. It's not an 'as if.' What I'm struggling to say is, it isn't any kind of metaphor. It starts as an encounter, and it continues as a relationship, and it's real."

The room became very quiet as William considered this. The night stepped down even deeper.

"So, can . . . I mean, could anyone . . . ?"

"Yes," said John.

Silence.

"How do you . . . ?"

"It's a matter of opening your heart. D' you remember—of

course you do; how could you forget?—when you came before our community the second time to ask admittance, and you spoke to us about letting your heart be seen? 'A casement that doesn't open easily,' I think you said. You opened it and let us see. It's much the same thing. In the spiritual realm, nothing can cross a threshold without permission, so Christ waits. But all you have to do is open the door of your heart and invite him to come in. He isn't passive. *Ecce sto ad ostium et pulso.* He waits and knocks—that means he is actively waiting to be invited."

"If I did this," William said slowly, "then Christ would expect of me . . . that I be patient with Oswald and spend time with him and take care of him, wouldn't he? Wouldn't he?"

In the darkness John smiled. "Aye, probably he would!"

"Can I get this quite clear? You're telling me that Jesus Christ is a living person who can be encountered as I am encountering you?"

"Yes," said John softly. "That's the implication of the resurrection and the ascension. Jesus lives beyond the dimensions we know. He is not subject to the limitations we experience. He died in a natural body and was raised in a spiritual body, and he now transcends the limitations of time and space and so can be with us always."

"Has there ever been anybody who invited him in and he did not come?"

"No," said John.

"Not even very sinful people?"

"We're all very sinful people. There is no difference. *Eum qui venit ad me, non ejiciam foras.*"

"Is there anything special you have to say when you ask him?"

"There is not."

"Does it have to be public? Do you have to tell anybody?"

"No. But it doesn't have to be secret either. It doesn't have to be anything apart from sincere."

When William spoke again, his words were so quiet John didn't catch what he said. "Sorry, what did you say?"

"I said I'd like to do that. I want to find the way into how you live and how Columba lived. When we came here—the way they looked at me—I was conscious again of your sheltering me. I want to find my way to how you do it, how you find that spaciousness and generosity of spirit and that deep core of peace; it seems to me to have something to do with this relationship you're describing. It's like a secret, an open secret, something that can't be seen except from the inside. From where I am, it just looks puzzling; it sounds unlikely. But if it's true . . . then I want it very much."

"Then ask him," said John, but he sounded sleepy now, and they lapsed into silence. After a while John snuggled down again and pulled the blankets up over his shoulders. Time passed. William listened to his abbot's breathing changing as, in the first faint lightening of the dawn, John drifted off to sleep.

William sat looking at the small square window set deep in the thick stone. He watched as the color of night began to give way to the morning.

"If you are there . . . " he whispered, then his voice faded into silence. He could not bear the idea that this might not be true, or even worse, that it might be true for others but not for him. Quietly, so as not to disturb John's sleep in this last brief hour before dawn, he slipped out of his bed and knelt on the floor of the guest chamber. He bent low, kneeling, his brow touching the floor, his hands cupped open before him, in the posture of a supplicant. "Jesus . . . Lord Jesus," he whispered, "I open my heart's door to you. My heart is open to you. Please come in. Please make yourself known to me, as you have to these others. Please forgive the man I have been and the choices I have made. There is so much to forgive, and it is late to begin again . . . but please may I do that? Even if I have to take care of Oswald, Lord Jesus, please come in to me."

William had no idea what he had been expecting: to see a figure of a man appear, to feel nothing at all but have faith in an answer, to experience a sense of another person in the room? But he was startled, when he got up from the floor as the sun rose, to experience a rising tide of joy more intoxicating than he would ever have thought possible, filling and flooding and saturating and overflowing his soul. And he knew—not believed, but knew without any shadow of doubting—that this was the presence of Jesus whom he had welcomed in.

He crept back into his bed and sat there very still. As the moments passed, he gradually became aware of another change. The impossible knot of blame and guilt lodged at the core of him had resolved. It had just gone. For as long as he could remember there had been this rooted tangle of things he had done wrong and things he thought he might have done wrong and things other people said he had done wrong even though he couldn't see why, grown into his being so that he could never get free of it. And it was all gone. For the first time in his life he felt peaceful and clean. William sat there, afraid to move in case this was only a momentary gift, and when the ordinary day began it would be trampled and sullied, everything back to normal. He knew that he should wake his abbot, for the sun was well risen, but he was afraid that if he said any word or took any step into the mundane, he might lose this place of transfiguration forever. The way he felt now might evaporate like a dream losing its identity to the waking day. John, undisturbed by the office bell here in the guest house, slept soundly. William sat in silence, life and joy so full he could hardly contain it stretching the boundaries of his heart. Then he began to feel guilty as he watched the morning sun rise higher, tipping over the sill of the window to strengthen the light in the room. When he heard Oswald begin to move about in the adjacent room, he knew it was time to get up. He let the glory fold down into the storehouse of his heart, such a precious, precious gift.

"Thank you, my Lord," he murmured softly. Then he slipped out of his bed, patted John firmly on the shoulder four or five times, and went to find out what help Oswald needed to begin the necessities of the day.

"What happened?" John asked later as they sat at table waiting for St. Olave's guest master to serve them with bread and ale, after they had washed and dressed.

Oswald turned his face to John, waiting alert and still to hear what might be amiss. William met his superior's gaze, and John observed the shyness, the reluctance to speak of experience too precious and deep for common talk across the table. He smiled. "You did it."

William nodded. "Yes, I did. I did."

Oswald asked a question, the content of which neither of them understood, but both of them guessed, and William turned his face away with a reluctant, hunted expression; he had no words for this. John realized that he was witnessing something outside his own experience and not quite within his comprehension: that these two men had managed to live in community together without coming either to know or to trust one another. It occurred to him that though St. Dunstan's may have reveled in luxury and licentiousness, it had known nothing of real friendship and could not have been a happy place, not even for those who benefited substantially from the considerable material successes it had enjoyed.

"He—may I say this, William?" John asked him, and William bowed his head in assent. "He has found his way through to touch the living presence of Christ for himself," said John, his voice quiet and reverent. "He has asked the Lord Jesus to abide in all fullness in his heart, and it is done."

Oswald remained entirely still, his face slightly puzzled. There had been no tradition at St. Dunstan's that could accommodate a real understanding of what John had just said.

The guest master came to their table and with civility, if not enthusiasm, gave them a jug of ale, a pat of butter, and a fragrant basket of bread rolls still hot from the oven. He had brought a cloth to protect Oswald's clothing, and from force of infirmary habit John rose to his feet to tie it on and serve Oswald his food.

"I'm sorry," said William quietly. "I should have done that."

An infirmarian learning to be an abbot, a superior learning to serve, a fastidious aristocrat learning to forget table manners in favor of survival: it was a strange fellowship, and the three of them bound in it found it hard to keep their feet in the paths of propriety and observe the rightful order of their going. But Christ was with them as they broke bread and shared what they had, as they made the best of what they had not and countered the coolness of their welcome with warmth of their own. Each of them felt Christ's presence, though Oswald knew only that he felt obscurely comforted.

Abbot John and Father William both felt glad to ride out of St. Olave's after Mass, though courteous thanks were expressed in their parting, and St. Olave's porter felt contrite enough to be uncommonly kind in his farewell.

They agreed on their road and traveled north into Derbyshire. The question of where they would sleep that night had determined their choice of direction: they headed for Doncaster. Their horses now well-fed and rested, an early start made it reasonable to suppose they could make that distance— just over thirty miles across country—in a day. Again William knew the Benedictine houses there better than John. There were more Cistercians than Benedictines in the north country now, but John wanted to knock only on a Benedictine door, to be sure the hospitality would be an obligation upon their hosts. He would not have either of his brothers turned away again. Living with the consequences of past misdeeds John saw as no bad thing; yet he disapproved in principle of any welcome that fell short of ordinary Christian kindness. So their road that day led to the small community of fifteen brothers at Loversall.

"I don't suppose they will," commented William.

"Will what?" They rode on in silence a little way, and John looked questioningly at William, who did not respond.

"Oh, I see! Love us all! No. But I expect they'll not take exception to Oswald and me—shame about you!" John teased him cheerfully.

"Too right," William replied. Then, "Father John . . . "

"Oh no. You've had an idea, haven't you?"

"I have."

"God preserve us; let's hear it then."

"Oswald, this concerns you and your eyes; so if you're feeling squeamish, put your hands over your ears."

John waited, curious as to what William had to say.

"It would take us not more than five miles out of our way to pass through Motherwell, would it?"

"That's right," John affirmed.

"Now, you said your sister and mother acted as midwives in their village for some years."

"They did." William heard the note of pride in John's voice. Both women had considerable skill in the healing arts.

"Midwifery. I have no personal experience of this, I hasten to add. I've never needed the services of a midwife. I've strayed from the straight and narrow every day of my life, but not in the direction of siring progeny."

"I'm relieved to hear it," replied Father John. "I should think one of you in the world is more than enough. So you don't need a midwife, and—?"

"But midwives . . . I imagine they need some skill in suturing from time to time, do they not?"

Abbot John digested this thought in silence. "Yes," he said slowly after a while; "yes, indeed they do. You are absolutely right. I would put money on Madeleine having a fair amount of experience in suturing wounds, not to mention cleaning hard-to-access mucous membranes. William, you're a genius. D' you know, I never thought of that! You *have* been filled with the Holy Spirit, haven't you?"

William cast him a withering, sidelong glance. "Anything you hadn't thought of must be beyond human wit, you mean?"

"Uh-huh. That's why they call me 'superior.' Motherwell it is. Can we make it up there by tomorrow, do you think?"

"No. Assuming we make Loversall tonight, the farthest we'll get tomorrow is Tadcaster. That's thirty miles and then some from Loversall. And it's the best part of another thirty miles on from Tadcaster to Motherwell. We shan't reach the Poor Clares until evening the day after tomorrow. I think we'll have to beg another night's lodging with them too. We can't push on any quicker than that because these two mounts won't take it—especially my poor palfrey with two of us up, even if you have both our packs. If we go for the greater distance, the horses will have to rest a day; it makes no odds. Still, we should be good for the extra night's lodging because, thanks to my divinely inspired intelligence, I had the gumption to check the chamber before we left and picked up the money bag you left behind on the bed. I'm surprised they don't call you 'inferior' if sagacity is the only criterion. What's that you say, Oswald? I'm sorry, without being able to see your face, I cannot make head nor tail of anything you just said. Think deeply, and divulge all your deliberations over our bread at midday. On second thought, that sounds slightly revolting."

The day was cloudy, bright and not too hot, so the horses journeyed easy. They stopped by the River Ryton, resting under the spreading canopy of a beech tree while their horses cropped the lush green grass of late spring and slaked their thirst in the shallows at the water's edge of that stopping place.

Their reception at Loversall Abbey, at the end of a long day, proved little different from what they had encountered in Chesterfield. Weary of surliness and suspicion, Abbot John thought he would be glad to see the moors again and climb the hill that led home. They made the best of it, kept to themselves, did what they could to minimize the mess Oswald generated, and slept soundly until the rising sun roused John and William early in the morning. They were on the road again after Mass, going gently to pace their mounts on this fifth day of traveling, making steady progress toward Tadcaster, where they asked shelter at a Cistercian house, because going on to a Benedictine community meant another five miles, and their horses were already turning questingly toward every quiet green spot. The Cistercian welcome seemed markedly reserved, but the travelers were admitted to the guest house with no awkward questions. A few raised eyebrows and astute glances in William's direction told John these men had grasped the situation; he was grateful when they chose to make no comment. For just the one night a truce could be reached, it seemed.

CHAPTER
FIVE

The following day took them on the road to Motherwell. They traveled in silence, their mood conditioned by John's palpable apprehension. While his abbot had been thanking the guest master at Tadcaster Abbey and making a gift of money in return for hospitality, William had discreetly explained to Father Oswald about Madeleine and Katelin. Oswald had listened with close attention, his face sad.

Nothing of the casual banter of the days before cheered this stretch of the journey. It merely seemed long. Tired and hungry, aching in body and low in spirit, they knocked for admittance as the first cool of evening made itself felt in the sunny afternoon. The shutter over the grating in the door slid back. "Abbot John! Father William! And someone we don't know! God bless you. Come on in!" The men felt comforted and encouraged by the first honest kindness that had met them so far.

"What brings you here? The sisters are in chapel. Is it Madeleine you seek? I'll ask Mother Mistress directly after they have finished Vespers if she may have permission to come to the parlor. Let me find you a bite to eat while you're waiting. Yes, don't you worry. We'll rub down the horses and see to their needs as well."

Sister Mary Cuthbert of the rosy and dimpled cheeks and smiling eyes, one of three extern sisters, betrayed no sign of shock at Oswald's appearance or his greeting. She took his hand in a brief squeeze of welcome and did not look away or even blink when his answering smile let loose a long drool of saliva, which he hastily wiped away with his other hand.

John could have kissed her, but he thought he'd better not.

Their mealtime routine was beginning to feel familiar. Oswald's arduous, hawking battle with his bowl of pottage seemed almost ordinary now. They had learned already how best to help him when help was needed—when to intervene and when to let him be.

"This honey tastes beautiful," commented John, adding some on top of the butter on his bread. "Would you like some, Father Oswald?"

"Don't give him honey!" protested William at the same time as Oswald eagerly assented.

"Why not?" John stopped in surprise, honey dripping from the spoon.

"'Why not?' What d' you mean, 'Why not?' Because honey is sticky and—oh, my Lord! Look, he's already got it on his sleeve, and it's dripped all down his scapular! Why do women insist on eating sweet food? Abbot John, you must need your head seeing to! For pity's sake! He can't even taste it! He didn't even know there *was* honey until you—"

"I *know!*" interrupted John. "William, I promise you this: if ever—God forbid—you lose your eyesight or your hearing or your mind, if ever you are paralyzed or cannot speak or your hand has a tremor—in any infirmary under my jurisdiction the brothers will understand that they are there to be your eyes, your hands, your ears. They will help you reach out for the choices you would have made but no longer can. They will know what those choices are because they'll have lived in community with you, known you and loved you. They will hold the cup steady for you, pick up the dropped spoon for you, mop up the spills for you. They will be your dignity, your comfort, your freedom, and, as far as it lies with them to be so, your happiness. While you're waiting for that day to come, you can take your turn at doing the same for somebody else who is living your tomorrow here today. I expect these sisters have a well; and from what I've seen so far, I think they will not begrudge us a bowl of water. Anyway, scapulars are made for honey and soup that didn't make it all the way. Why d'you think we have them? And women eat sweet food because it tastes good. I like honey too."

William said nothing to this. He watched Father Oswald defiantly clinging on to his bread and butter and honey, enjoying it. The taste was not there for him anymore, but he could still smell it; and it belonged to the memory of past pleasures. John grinned at William as he watched the greasy, sugary mess transfer inexorably to Oswald's hands and sleeves and face, and even his hair. William shook his head in disbelief as the table around Oswald's plate began to reflect the rays of the sinking sun.

"Jesus," said John. "It's Jesus."

William looked at him. "What is?"

His abbot's eyes searched his, playfully, kindly. "This. This whole thing. Finding the grace to take what is truly awful and make it sing again. Identifying something in a ruined life that still can be sweet even if you can't taste it anymore. Come on, William! Don't begrudge him his bread and honey."

"These women have taken us in," William replied after pondering this. "They have shown us the first real friendliness of anyone. Do we not owe them some consideration? What will they think of us?"

"They will think," said his abbot, "that we love our brother. *'These women'* gave us the honey."

Sister Mary Cuthbert trod purposefully into the room, bearing a large, steaming bowl of hot water. Over her arm she had a number of linen towels.

"The sisters are finished in chapel, and I've sent word to

dear Mother," she said briskly. "I thought you might like the chance to refresh yourselves after your supper. Are you all finished? Or would you like some more?"

They all three thanked her, Oswald's shining face beaming in hideous but heartfelt gratitude. John began to laugh as he started the process of restoring Oswald to any kind of respectable appearance. The extent of the mess Oswald had created released the tension of his dread at meeting his sister after last time. As he tackled the mayhem, he found himself helpless with laughter. "Oh, glory, *you* do it!" he said to William, handing him the cloth.

Oswald sat patiently still, his face lifted to be cleaned, his hands held clear of whatever unseen chaos he had unwittingly created. As he wiped away the stickiness and the adhering crumbs, William found himself drawn in to both the comedy and the pathos of the moment. Sister Mary Cuthbert had brought enough towels. It took ten minutes, but William restored both the man and his environment to a state of complete order and cleanliness, while his abbot stood watching, leaning against the wall, his arms folded, his eyes full of laughter.

"And no, you can't have seconds!" said William to his now perfectly respectable brother. Then, "Oswald," he added seriously, "please will you forgive me?"

They went from the guest house to the parlor, where someone had hung a lantern on either side of the grille. Three stools stood there now. John's lightheartedness visibly evaporated as soon as they walked through the door into the austere little room. William guided Oswald to the stool in the middle of the three. They took their seats in silence and waited.

Presently the door in the convent wall, on the other side of the room, opened. John half stood, but sat down again as Madeleine came in with averted eyes and stony expression, taking her seat without coming to the grille to greet them. She didn't even look at them. Her face was pale and formidably pensive. She had grown thin. John felt decidedly unsure of his welcome.

"Wes hal, brother." She used the old country greeting as the nervous silence continued. She directed her words to John, but her tone did not embody the kindness of the Old English words, which meant *be thou whole*. She looked at him then for the first time, her eyes dark and unfriendly. "You asked to see me."

Oswald remained completely still, his face watchful, his whole body reading the uneasy atmosphere of the interaction. William looked at the floor. He felt wretched for John, but thought that in this one he had neither place nor power to intervene.

John stood up and went to the grille. Madeleine did not move except that she appeared almost imperceptibly to lean backwards. She did not want him close.

He had put his hands to the bars, but fearing that this might seem too insistent and intrusive, he moved them to rest lightly on the wooden beam in which the iron railings were set. For a brief moment he wondered whether to pursue the usual courtesies of asking after her health and how everything was going, but he quickly recognized the pointlessness of trying to initiate any such exchange. She sat steadfastly on her stool, enduring being there, staring straight ahead, but not at him. "Madeleine," he said, "we need your help."

He had her attention then. With a slight, puzzled frown she said, "*My* help? With what?"

"My brothers here are new to our community," he explained. "They were Augustinians from a priory near Chesterfield. Their house was torched and the brothers killed—trapped in the fire. These two escaped. Father William, who was their prior—that's their superior, for theirs was a priory, not an abbey—found his way to us. He traveled through the same country as I did on my way home from the university at Cambridge, and at the same time. Mercifully he reached us, and we took him in. Father Oswald I met in Chesterfield, destitute, on my travels home from the university. I could not take him with me. No, forgive me; that's not true. I *did* not take him with me, for I was in haste to return before Easter and did not want to be slowed by the difficulty, for those who might offer me lifts, of an extra body to accommodate. I left him in Chesterfield, but I told Father William I had seen him. Since I reached home, my feet have hardly touched the ground; there has been so much to learn and tackle from the start. And I have been . . . the news of what had befallen you and Mother . . . it . . . I was . . . oh, never mind it, I am not excusing myself. I was remiss, and if I had not been, this would never have happened.

"After I came to see you here last time, Father William approached me to ask if we might go back to Chesterfield to search for the brother I left behind. So we went, and by God's grace we found him. But, Madeleine, they have hurt him grievously—cut out most of his tongue and put out his eyes, as you see. He has been living in the mire and muck of the street, left to see to his wounds by himself with nobody to help him. I thank God he is in no worse state, but he cannot be left as he is now. Sister, I have never stitched anyone's eyelids. I have watched surgery but never done it. I do not have the experience I need, and I am afraid of hurting him. His sockets are mucky from the street. Father William thought that you might have the skills to help us. I know you are not eager to see me, but I don't know of anywhere else to turn."

Madeleine listened carefully to this, and William raised his head to watch her response. When John stopped speaking, she looked at her brother very levelly.

"What a pity you did not go back," she said coldly. Involuntarily, as he saw John flinch, both of William's hands tightened into fists, not in aggression but in unbearable tension. He felt the hurt of her words harrow their way through every level of John's soul, so that for a moment he could not answer.

Then, "I did go back, Madeleine," he said quietly, humbly. "But can we leave me and my shortcomings to one side for now? I am not unaware of my faults and my omissions. Will you help us? Have you the skills?"

Madeleine sat without moving a moment longer. William saw in her face a deep reluctance, as if wherever her soul had hidden away it had no desire at all to be drawn forth into the turbulence of human need and frailty. Finally, "Let me see," she said. She stood, crossed the room to lift the lantern down from its hook, and came forward to the grille. She was standing so close to John then, but she did not touch him or smile at him or even look at him. She stood waiting for Oswald to come forward to her, her face closed and remote.

The parlor was not a big room. Only six short, hesitating, shuffling steps took Oswald to the grille, holding his hands before him, groping as he moved toward her voice. William moved with him, his hand cupped under Oswald's elbow to steer him to the right place.

"Don't do it like that," said Madeleine calmly, observing their progress toward her. William's eyes met hers as they came to the grille. John thought somewhere in one universe or another he heard the clash of steel on steel as two swords met.

"Like what?" asked William in a voice entirely devoid of warmth.

"When you walk with a blind man, you should let *him* take *your* arm, and you lead him. At the moment, *you're* taking *his* arm and steering him. He can't see where to go, so you are making him too vulnerable, in reality as well as in how he feels. If you let *him* take *your* arm instead, he will feel more secure, and you will progress more effectively."

"Thank you," said William. "I shall remember," he added in a voice like frostbite.

As Oswald stood at the grille, Madeleine paused one final moment, in which she seemed to be summoning the reserves of her spirit for this encounter. Then she put her left hand through the railings and took hold of Oswald's chin, holding the lantern high so she could see as she moved his face to this angle and that.

"Open your mouth," she said. "By heaven, they did not leave you much, did they? Adam, where's your handkerchief?"

Without thinking, she used her brother's baptismal name, and he moved to wipe the saliva that ran from Oswald's mouth.

"Thank you. I've seen what I need to," she said abruptly. "Sit down."

John returned miserably to his seat. Madeleine watched as William proffered his arm. Oswald slipped his hand through and was led easily back to his stool. "That's better," she remarked. She hung the lantern back on its hook and sat down.

"We shall need some dwale," she said, "and I do not know at all if Sister Bede has the ingredients. For one thing we need the gall of a boar—not of a gilt—which should be fresh. It can be obtained when a beast is butchered, but it's a matter of finding who has one and when they will be slaughtering. Certainly they owe me more than a few favors in the village, and I think there will be those who would be right glad to do what they might think will appease me, since I am alive and possessed of an excellent memory. I had not meant to disclose that I am here though; what if they come for me again? If they know the community is harboring me, the safety of the whole house might be put in jeopardy. Anyway, I can ask in our infirmary, but I'm sure that will be one ingredient we are lacking. Of course, Sister Thomas might be willing to slaughter our boar, but it'll mean we have to buy another, else we'll have no piglets, and they do us well for a steady bit of income. I'll ask her, but be prepared to accept that she might say no. In similar wise I have not seen hemlock in Sister Bede's dispensary, but I can look, and I know where we can get it if she has none." Madeleine frowned, considering the situation. The challenge it presented had rekindled the habit of a lifetime's healing work, in spite of the trauma that had locked her soul away. She had been a healer far longer than she had been a broken victim, and the roots of familiarity grew deep. "Bryony, vinegar, henbane, and lettuce we have," she continued. "Once I can mix the dwale, I am willing to proceed. Without it, I will not. I am changed now. I cannot bear to hurt him, stitching without medicine. Brother—"

She suddenly stopped in what she was saying to John, as if some pestering thing had finally caught her attention, and turned her gaze very directly toward William, searching his eyes with hers. "What's the *matter* with you? Are you angry with me for some reason? You have never met me before, except only the once, but you look as though you hate me."

His composure unruffled by this bald confrontation, William considered her calmly. "I think I do not hate you," he said thoughtfully, "though at this moment I admit it, I am not far off." His eyes assayed her unhurriedly. "I am not angry. Something has to be important to arouse anger. I have seen enough to know that none of us is in any real sense important. But it offends me—and hurts me, I confess—to watch you torture your brother. He has been good to me. He has saved my life, sheltered me from violence and deserved animosity. Last time we were here you walked out and left a sobbing heap of pulverized humanity for me to pick up, and I see you are ready with another lashing this evening. You have been through hell? So have I. So has Oswald. Get over it. It wasn't John's fault. He wasn't there for you? Nay, nor was I, nor any other man. He is your brother, not your husband. Since you ask."

Madeleine's lips tightened as he spoke until they were bloodless. "Did I hear it said that you wanted my help?" she asked after a moment, her voice hard. The question hung in the air as a threat. William faced it with equilibrium.

"Aye, but not enough to grovel for it, nor yet to stand aside while you punish somebody who never hurt you, because you have run away from those who did."

His cool gaze held hers. His eyebrows lifted. "Are you going to tell us now that Oswald can go through a fresh hell because I answered your straight question with a straight answer and your *amour propre* has taken a bit of a tumble?"

John rubbed his brow, looking slightly desperate. "Stop it, William," he said. "Please stop it. If I can get the gall and the hemlock—if you will tell me where to ask—will you help us, Madeleine? Please. Not for me, not for William; God knows he has enemies all over England. Just for these poor, swollen eye sockets that need protection from dirt and flies, and to give this man some dignity back and clothe him with compassion. Madeleine? Please. Don't let the whole of life be about people hurting each other simply because they can. I will seek out the things you need without letting anyone know you are here."

"Please help me," Oswald enunciated as clearly as he could, and that brought silence.

"I will ask tonight about the hemlock and the pig. If the answer is no, you must go and search out gall and hemlock at first light, Adam, so I can mix the dwale in the morning. Then we shall have good midday light to work with. I will make a room ready with everything else we need. And, Adam, if you are wise, you will take Sister Mary Cuthbert with you if you need to go into the village to ask for a pig—and leave this William behind. The people love Mary Cuthbert. She does not antagonize them."

John's eyes met hers. "*Father* William," he said very softly.

The faintest smile touched Madeleine's face, but not her eyes. "Ah, yes, *Father*," she said, "to show I respect him."

Oswald sat as he was, his head cocked and his body motionless, still using every sense he had to feel the dynamics of the conversation. William bent his head, withdrawing from the interaction, for which he had no further use. John looked steadily at his sister. In a movement so slight it was hard to discern, he shook his head. Seeing it, the assurance in her face faltered a little.

"I will ask dear Mother's permission before Compline for all we have discussed," said Madeleine less truculently, "but I cannot think she will refuse us. Except maybe the pig. I hope you will join us for Compline if you are not too tired. Other than that, God give you good night, Father John, Father Oswald, *Father* William."

William looked up then, and John was surprised and relieved to catch a flash of amusement pass between them. For his own part, though he saw confrontation to be occasionally necessary and bravely faced, he never enjoyed it; it was never a game. But he recognized that he had witnessed an odd apology given and accepted.

Mother Mary Beatrix gave her permission for their enterprise and spoke briefly to Abbot John before Compline to affirm this was so. "Madeleine has explained that the gall of a boar is necessary to make the medicine needful for the procedure she must do. I understand that your time is precious, Father John, and I will not hear of your walking the country round about in search of an animal for slaughter when we have one in our own orchard. It is the least we can do for your poor brother priest who has been so savagely hurt. We will gladly give you our pig, and Sister Mary Cuthbert will be going straight after first Mass to the cottage of the man who looks after the butchering of animals for us. Madeleine has told me that all should be ready for when the sun is at its height, and so it shall be."

"Dear Mother, how can I thank you for your kindness? You

must at least let us pay you for the pig—no, really you must. We will give you what is necessary to replace a boar good for breeding. God reward you. We are so very grateful."

It felt strange to sit in the nave of the church while the community gathered in the choir. For so many years his stall in choir had been an essential part of home to John. On his travels when he had to beg hospitality, if he stayed at a monastery he would usually find a community of men. He had stayed with nuns before but very rarely. Even so, though he sat in the parishioners' benches in the nave, he felt welcome, and the generosity and loving-kindness of these sisters warmed his heart.

"We can begin to set you right again now, my brother," said John to Father Oswald as they retired to the guest house when the last prayers were said and the *Salve Regina* sung. "This will protect your sockets and make you look tidy. Do you know what the dwale is?"

Oswald shook his head.

"'Tis a medicine that will send you to sleep while we do the stitching, so that we shall not hurt you as we work. And when you wake up, its effects will gentle any soreness there is at first. So you will not feel what we do."

"Thank you!" Oswald used the sign language of the Silence, and for extra emphasis he pressed his palms together and bowed his face to his fingertips.

After he had seen Oswald safely and comfortably into his bed, though they were now in silence John crossed the long room to the bed on which William sat unlacing his boots.

"Yes, Father? You wanted to talk?"

"Coming in?"

"Only for a moment. I want to beg your pardon for my sister. This is not like her. She is the kindest, most joyous soul. I think the savagery worked upon her has driven her into a place she cannot come back from. Though mind you, she has always been very forthright, very direct in both question and comment. That's the healer's way; you have to be. My mother was the same."

"Candid suits me," replied William, "and I've no doubt she and I can find our way to some sort of accommodation. You need have no dread there will be fisticuffs when we go into the enclosure tomorrow. But . . . " He hesitated, then said, completely serious now, "I owe you so much. It was more than I could do to stand by and see those barbed arrows find their mark in your heart. Beyond that, she can say what she likes about me. Why should I care?"

John nodded. "Go gently though, in the way you answer her. Take the long view. The day will arrive eventually when she emerges out of this state of mind and comes to terms with all that befell her. When she finds her new equilibrium, she will have forgotten she was so hard, for my guess is, she does not feel hard inside, only hurt and beleaguered. I think the pain she inflicts is a measure of the pain she feels. Our part is to understand and be forgiving. If I can receive patiently the hurt she dishes out, that may wick it away from her soul a little and help her recover. If I recognize what is happening, it makes it easy for me to forgive. The thing we have to hold before us is the remembrance that this is a molten time when new things are forged. If we offer her gentleness and understanding now, we can forge healing. If we meet what she dishes out with resentment and indignation, we shall forge enmity, when what is in flux cools into the new way she will be. Am I . . . do you grasp what I mean?"

"Father John," replied William, "as I travel with you, I am surprised by finding myself grateful for the day St. Dunstan's burned down. I am proud to be a son of your house." As he looked at him, his eyes shone with admiration. "Go to bed. We have work to do in the morning."

John smiled.

"A son of my house? Ha! Any other brother would stand respectfully until *I* told *him* to go to bed! Nay, that's no rebuke! Sleep well. Until the morning."

✠   ✠   ✠

The light came streaming glorious through the east window above the choir altar as the three men sat in the parish side of the chapel waiting for the morrow Mass to begin after Prime. John and William watched Sister Mary Cuthbert as the mother abbess came to stand there, evidently with something to communicate.

She listened and nodded and, as Mother Mary Beatrix returned to her stall, Mary Cuthbert in barefoot silence came back from the sanctuary to whisper to William, who sat at the end of the bench, "Dear Mother says she has asked of Sister Bede, and she has the hemlock." If Mary Cuthbert felt any surprise at passing this message, her face did not betray it. "And she says that unless you tell her otherwise, she will let our parish priest know that Abbot John will celebrate first Mass for us tomorrow morning."

John, listening also, caught the quiet words and nodded his assent.

"God reward you; we are honored," Mary Cuthbert murmured, smiling as she left them to prepare their hearts and minds for the Eucharist.

She returned as Mass ended to stand respectfully near the bench where they sat, ready to escort them into the enclosure.

Oswald took William's arm, and they followed Mary Cuthbert into the Lady Chapel. She took them to a door, insignificant in appearance but securely locked, adjacent to the sanctuary. She drew from under her scapula a bunch of keys of impressive size and quickly selected the right one to open the door. With a nod and a smile, she stood aside to let them through into the enclosure, then closed the door behind them, and they heard her turn the key.

While the enclosure door near the parlor would have allowed them into the claustral living quarters of the sisters, the way through the Lady Chapel took them out into a rose garden, in leaf but not yet in bloom at this time of year. For a moment John could hardly see as he emerged from the cool dimness of the chapel into the spring morning rioting with birdsong and dazzling sunlight.

In only a minute Madeleine appeared around the tall yew hedge to find them. "Wes hal, fathers. I trust you slept well?"

John felt relieved to find her manner less cold, if still reserved. He could sense the intense focus of her energy as she held herself in readiness for what she had to do. For now at least, her mind was no longer haunted by vivid memories of trauma, nor preoccupied with anger, terror, or distress; just for this day she was a skilled healer again, responding to someone else's pain with a lifetime's mastery of knowledge and practice.

"If you will follow me, the infirmary lies up yonder slope, just at the end of this path and at the foot of the hill that leads up to the burial ground. We are all prepared. Sister Thomas shed tears for her pig, but she brought me the gall bladder in a bowl, and the bile is mixed in with the rest."

As they came to the low infirmary building, built of the same honey-colored stone as St. Alcuin's, Madeleine stopped, looking up to see the lark whose song she could hear in trilling cascades as it climbed into the dizzy blue of the cloudless sky. "'Tis so high! Can you see it, Adam?" She forgot her stance of aloofness as her eye searched out the bird, habits of joy in life and easy familiarity for that moment reasserting themselves, bringing back the person she had always been. Oswald stood listening, his head tilted to one side, while John and William squinted up with Madeleine into the brightness of the heaven.

William shaded his eyes with his hand, his head tipped

back as he stood entranced, watching the bird mount up and up and up, always singing. All his life he had loved the wild freedom of the rising flight of the lark. Enthralled, he did not notice as Madeleine recalled herself to the purpose of her visit, leaving the spilling exuberance of music to the sweetness of blue. "What?" he said defensively when his attention returned to what they were about and realized Madeleine was observing him with focused curiosity.

"Round your neck," she said quietly, "you have a faint mark. Have you been hanged?"

Oswald became totally still at those words. John moved in sudden consternation. "Oh God!" said William, brought sharply back to earth. "It never pays to let your vigilance slip for an *instant*, does it? *Anywhere!*"

For the first time since he had known him, John saw William obviously and completely caught off his guard. "Yes, I have been hanged," he ground out bitterly, resenting the intrusion of the question, "but not by the hand of others."

"You tried to hang yourself?"

John wished Madeleine would not pursue this, but the question was asked now. Oswald remained completely still, his apprehensions about the hour ahead forgotten. He'd had no inkling before this of anything that had happened to William after St. Dunstan's fire.

"How else do you think anyone hangs who is not hung by somebody else?"

"Oh, plenty of ways! There are all manner of accidents. But not in your case? And this was quite recent, I see, or you would not still have the mark. Maybe six weeks ago?"

"Aye, about that. Madam, I will answer as many impertinent questions as you have to fire at me later when we have leisure. But while the sun is high, should we not remember what we are here to do?"

"Indeed. In any case, though I perceive you might taste acid in anyone's mouth, I can find no whiff of despair about you now. The thing that drove you to this act—it is healed then?"

John looked aside, acutely embarrassed by her persistence, but William looked her in the eye. "It is healed," he answered her. "I have shelter from the storm."

She nodded, satisfied for the moment. "That's well then," she said briskly, "so we don't have to worry about *you*. Let's go to our task, as you say. Sister Bede has lit us a fire. I know it's hot, but Father Oswald must be really warm. The more he has to make him drowsy, the less hemlock I need to put in. The less hemlock I put in, the less likelihood I shall kill him by mistake. To this end I have begged from Sister Paul a slug of mead to mix in with the wine—and the wine is sweet and heady anyway."

John saw that though Oswald stood quietly, the mention of a possibility of killing him registered in his face. Though years of monastic discipline enabled him to retain composure, his hands half-hidden from view at his sides in the folds of his habit began clenching and unclenching despite his best efforts to appear relaxed.

"Don't be afraid: my sister's bedside manner has more terror than kindness," John joked gently, putting his hand on Oswald's back, stroking him in a soothing motion that brought a sudden shaky sigh from Oswald as the anxiety decreased a fraction. "You will be in good hands. It is better for you to sleep through this. Don't be afraid. I shall be with you. And while you sleep, and Madeleine and I work on your eyes, William and all these good sisters will hold you fast in their prayers. Don't be afraid."

Oswald nodded. He lifted his hand to wipe away saliva that he felt trickling. John saw that his hand was trembling.

"Let's get to it then. Come inside," said Madeleine, who had also seen the signs of dread. "Yes, you too, Father William, you might be useful. I cannot think that much disturbs *you*."

William looked at her, hesitating. "Not much," he said, "but

I confess if I have to watch what you are about to do, I am likely to pass out. I cannot. . . . Well; no, thank you."

For the first time an impish grin suddenly lit Madeleine's face. "Squeamish, eh? Stay out here then! Come, Adam; come, Oswald; let's get this done."

Abbot John let Father Oswald take his arm and, leading him, followed Madeleine into the infirmary. Though the day was warm, for this occasion Sister Bede had kept her infirmary charges in their rooms. Priests were not to be troubled by the uninvited presence of her sisters. She stood ready in an inner room, where the fire had been burning since morning. Madeleine and Sister Bede had prepared the room together while John went in search of what they needed. A bed stood near the window, through which a strong shaft of sunlight shone. Two uncompromising Franciscan pillows topped by a third, a soft goose-down pillow, had been set ready. "We can't let him lie flat on his back without a complete tongue," Madeleine remarked. At the foot of the bed, a table had been spread with a clean fair linen cloth. On it they had laid out a small bowl and four large bowls covered with cloths, a tidy pile of lint scraps, fine silk and needles for suturing, two short, slender knives, a low stack of neatly folded linen towels, a stoppered flask and a beaker both of forest glass, the beaker empty, the flask half-full of something red. The rays of sun from the window sparkled on the glass and lit ruby glints in the contents of the flask. Warming on the hearth stood a pitcher of wine, its aromatic fumes permeating the air of the room along with the pleasant fragrance of wood smoke. Sister Bede held in her hands a second stoppered flask two-thirds full of dark liquid.

"You have used the exact measures I said?" asked Madeleine. "He is thin; we must not give too much."

"Exactly as you instructed, Sister," the infirmarian replied.

"God reward you. Now the challenge will be for him to swallow it. It does not have to go down too fast, thankfully. Father

Oswald, we need this drink to go down without choking you, so I will not administer it, you must do it yourself. Don't fret if you dribble some, it doesn't matter. We shall know when you have had what you need, for you will start to drowse."

She took the pitcher of wine from the fireside and poured some into the glass on the table to just over half-full. "Now, Sister Bede, add from your flask until the glass is comfortably full," she instructed. "There, that's enough."

She set the pitcher back by the fireside and took the glass to Oswald. "Wash your hands, Father John," she said, careful to use his name in religion in the presence of Sister Bede, who valued respect. The infirmarian set her flask on the table and uncovered one of the four large bowls, into each of which had been poured boiling water now cooled to be comfortably hot. The small bowl held wine for cleaning Oswald's eye sockets. John smelled the pungent fragrance of lavender and conifer oils in the steam as he washed his hands thoroughly, using the nail brush set beside the bowl. Sister Bede took from him the towel he had used when he had dried his hands.

Meanwhile Oswald, under Madeleine's watchful eye, was making a success of swallowing the dwale. He used a peculiar tossing of his head to get the liquid down; because there were no solids incorporated into it, the technique was simple and effective.

"Well done," said Madeleine quietly as he continued to drink. "That's right," she murmured softly. "Good lad . . . well done, my brother . . . " And as she continued to speak to him softly, the three of them watched his head nod and his body start to sway. Madeleine had her hand around his as his grasp relaxed and let go of the glass. "Now!" she said without raising her voice. Sister Bede took his legs at the knees, and Madeleine took him under the shoulders. They lifted him across the small room and onto the bed. John watched, holding his hands, now completely clean, clear of everything.

As Sister Bede positioned Oswald on the bed, Madeleine hastily but thoroughly scrubbed her hands in the aromatic water of the second large bowl. "Pick up the lint pieces, Adam," she said, forgetting Sister Bede's sense of etiquette. "Sister, bring the bowl of wine."

One by one she took the scraps from John, and he watched as she cleaned the sockets meticulously, first one and then the other, ensuring that all was thoroughly cleansed and not the smallest speck of a foreign body left inside. Everything she did was swift but unhurried, every movement deft and neat. Observing her, John saw she had forgotten herself, forgotten the horrors of recent memory—everything except the task in hand. As she worked, she dropped each used scrap of lint on the floor at her feet. When the pile in John's hands was down to three scraps remaining, she stepped quickly back to the table, washed her hands again in the third large bowl, and dried them on the third towel, dropping that too on the floor.

She took up the first of the two needles threaded with the silk, and John watched her clever fingers in admiration as she made the neatest job of suturing Oswald's left eye. "Pick up one of the blades for me, Adam, from the table," she said when she was done. He brought her the very sharp scalpel set there, and she cut the thread, dropping the blade into one of the bowls in which she had washed her hands. Then she scrubbed and dried them a third time, took up the second silk, and sutured the right eye. John was ready with the second blade as she completed the stitching. She cut the thread, dropped the blade in the bowl with its fellow, washed her hands in the water she had last used, and dried her hands on one of the two remaining towels in the stack.

She came back to Oswald's side. "We just wipe off with wine now for good measure," she said. "You do one. I'll do the other." She took one of the two scraps John still held, dipped it in the bowl of wine in Sister Bede's hands, and wiped the left eye carefully from center to tail. John did the same with the right eye.

"Now we wake him up. Give me that last scrap of lint."

Madeleine took the stoppered flask of red liquid from the table. "This is vinegar and water—God reward you, Sister; you can put that bowl of wine down now and pick up the discarded cloths from the floor."

Splashing the vinegar and water on Oswald's temples, Madeleine spoke his name several times. He closed his mouth, which had fallen open as he slept, and began to murmur incoherently. "Oswald! Speak to me!" said Madeleine sharply in a voice of command not to be ignored, and Oswald obediently responded with some blurred and incomprehensible reply.

She looked satisfied. "That's all I need. Well, that went without a hitch! He can stay in here until he is fit to stand and walk. By Vespers he should be able to return to the guest house. Abbot John was an infirmarian, Sister Bede; this man will be safe in his care. Can I leave the two of you now to clean up in here and bring him out into the fresh air as soon as he is ready?"

She washed her hands one last time and dried them on the last remaining towel, leaving it on the table for John to do the same if he wished, then went out into the sunshine. "We are done; all is well," she said to William who watched her approach, his expression intent in expectation of her report. "They are tidying up and tending to him. Would you care to walk up the hill a little? I need to feel the breeze on my face. It's hot in there."

William did not reply but got up from the low wall on which he had been sitting and went with her up the grassy track that led toward their burial ground. Madeleine glanced at him as they walked together. "What has been happening—exactly, I mean? I heard what my brother said last night," she asked as they strolled up the path. The scent of chamomile was sharp on the warm air.

"Happening?"

"To you, that you tried to take your life—and to Oswald? I have not put together a full picture."

William sighed. "To tell you the truth, I am almost weary of the tale." He plucked a stem from a tall weed that grew by the path and toyed with it, pulling the leaves off one by one, rolling them between his fingers. "Well, then, our community—and I as its prior—we were not loved; we were not gentle; we were not charitable. We made enemies, and they burned our house. Oswald—oh, but you can see what happened. He escaped the fire, but he was seen by those who had a grudge against us. They thought they'd teach him a lesson since they hadn't succeeded in burning him to death."

Madeleine stole a glance at his face, hearing the savage bitterness that came into his voice as he contemplated what had been done to Oswald. Set and pale, not even noticing her face turn toward him, ripping the remaining little leaves from the plant stem, he continued, "First they put out his eyes, after a violent scuffle; he has told me all this as we've traveled, but his speech is so poor it has taken a while to understand. That—the eyes—did in his inclination to resist anything else they had in mind. He thinks they did not want him to recognize them. Next they used him much as you were used and gelded him as well just to make their point. He thought he was beyond caring by then and imagined with one last kick they would leave him alone with his agony, but no. One of them had the bright idea he might try to tell the tale. To ensure he did not, they thought they'd leave him with no means to do so. That was Oswald, then. What's left of him you can see for yourself. He seems to me to have come through with surprising fortitude and resilience. I wouldn't have guessed he had it in him.

"And me? I was afraid for my life and was welcome nowhere.

I tried house after house, and they would not let me in. When I finally came to St. Alcuin's, I was hated there as thoroughly as anywhere. They knew me from former days. I had used their abbot ill. I guess you remember him. He was a crippled man. I was not kind to him. The community had no mind to give me refuge. Your brother, God bless him, did what he could to plead for me, but they remained, all but a few, indifferent. It was my only hope, you understand, or I would not have gone there. I did not expect they would have forgotten how I'd used their Father Columba. So nowhere was safe. I thought I'd better finish it before I fell into rougher hands and found myself tortured and beaten and maimed. But Brother Thomas—though he loathed me with every fiber of his being and has never hesitated to let me know it—found me swinging and cut me down, and here I am. They let me stay. That's it."

They walked on in silence.

"Did you . . . did you really deserve—either of you—anything of this?"

William stopped and looked at her frankly. "Aye, we did." Then he carried on walking. "We surely did. But it was not the fire nor the hatred nor the fear that made me sorry for it—but that Thomas saved my life without stopping to think, for all he hated me, and that John did what he could to shelter me from every well-earned punishment, and that Michael sat up all night to pull me through when I had pneumonia and would have come out of the safety of those walls with me if they had still turned me away. I saw in them something that puzzled me. Something beyond what I have encountered anywhere else. It is a connection with Christ. So I . . . "

"Yes?" Intrigued, Madeleine, looking sideways at him, saw his shyness, the faint color that rose in his cheeks. "What?" she said.

"I opened my heart to Christ," William mumbled. "I invited him in."

"You are shy about this? Is it not what every brother does?" William laughed. "No, it's not. And yes, I am. It feels very private. Despite what you see, Madeleine, I am not entirely hard boiled. Somewhere at the core something still is alive, which must imply some kind of sensitivity—some vital nerve still sensible to love and fear and pain. But I protect it as best I can."

"You mean you still have a soul?"

Again he stopped in his tracks, and she was surprised to see as he looked at her that the question had found and touched that nerve. "I hope so," he whispered.

"I hope so too," she answered, offering him a way out of the space of vulnerability he found himself in, "or else you would be just like a woman—for the theologians among you monks say, do they not, that women have no souls?"

William's eyes met the challenge of her gaze, no irony in them now. "They do say so," he admitted, "but I don't know why. For you know and I know it is not true. Maybe they would not say it if they had met you."

Further surprised by this unexpected gentleness, Madeleine turned back to their path and walked on. She felt puzzled. Even with every receptor in her being questing to test the presence of this monk walking at her side, she could not find what had seemed so obnoxious to her in him last night. Detachment was what she felt now—he wanted nothing from her. But she found also an obscure conviction that she could entirely trust him. In these intuitions she could not remember an instance where she had been wrong. No further conversation passed between them as they climbed to the brow of the hill, after which the path dipped before the land began to rise again beyond the wall of the burial ground.

"We should go back in a minute. I must check on Father Oswald and see that all is well." As they reached the burial ground, Madeleine turned back toward the monastery buildings at the foot of the hill. "Oh, look—there's my brother. Oswald is not with him. I think they will have put him to bed. I guess Adam wanted to visit Mother's grave again while he's here."

John crossed from the infirmary to the foot of the track they had climbed. He had seen them and waved back as Madeleine waved down to him. She watched his easy stride as he started to walk up the grassy path.

William sat down to wait for him on the grass in the sunshine, resting his back against the stones of the burial ground wall. Madeleine sat down beside him, not too near.

"Do you really want to be a Poor Clare nun?" he asked her suddenly. Madeleine did not need to turn the question over in her mind very long.

"No," she said honestly, "but I really want to be safe."

He took this in thoughtfully and did not immediately reply. He felt her observing every detail of him—his hands, one folded peacefully on the other, his forearms resting on top of his drawn-up knees, then her gaze traveling on from the long bony fingers, noting their shape and structure, to his feet, dusty in well-worn sandals, and the rough, faded black of his tunic. "Didn't they give you a new habit when you joined?" she asked.

He glanced sideways at her. "Not much gets past you, does it? I asked if I could keep this one. You will have known Abbot Columba, I think? This was his."

"You mean Father Peregrine?"

"Yes, him. It was his."

"I thought you didn't like him. You said you used him ill."

"That's why I wanted to keep it. At first the thought of putting it on scared me. Now what I feel is that I am wearing his forgiveness. Look, Madeleine, why don't you come and live with us?"

Startled, she looked at his face, wondering if she had heard aright and, if she had, if he really meant it. "What? How could I? I'm a woman," she said, "and you live in a monastery."

He turned his head, and the cool gaze of his pale eyes met hers.

"Aye, but we have much more land than that. There is a cottage in the close wanting a tenant. I think we would not go hungry without its rent. You'd like it. The garden is bursting with herbs already, and there's space for a henhouse."

Madeleine felt such a gripping of hope around her heart in that moment, she could hardly breathe. She was afraid to reach out for this possibility in case it should be snatched away.

"Is there room for goats?" she asked tentatively, playing for time.

William laughed, and she watched the crinkling of the skin at the corner of his eyes. "No," he said, "but I think we could find you a place to tether a goat on our land. You would not be vulnerable there as you are here. Motherwell is a small place, and the people do not travel. They will be ignorant and unaware of your connections. I'll wager John might as well have gone to the moon when he left for St. Alcuin's—am I right?"

"That was the problem," said Madeleine softly. "He was just *gone*. That was all they knew. But won't it be the same anywhere? Your village is not big either. Won't they think I am a witch and a heretic by St. Alcuin's too?"

"No. They will think you are the abbot's sister, and you will have the sense to come every day to Mass and to Vespers, so they will know you are devout."

William saw the struggle in her face. He saw that she wanted this, but something stood in the way. "What? Tell me," he said.

Madeleine felt again the unlikely sense that she could trust him, whoever he was and whatever he had done.

"It was important to Mother that we did not impose on Adam. He is protective and kind by nature. She said we must let him go and never breathe a word of what it cost us. If I stay here, I will not become a burden to him." This was not an admission easily made. She and Katelin had kept their understanding entirely to themselves.

"If you stay miserable, you will destroy him!" replied William. He shot her a sly, sideways glance. "Besides, the brothers at St. Alcuin's are good and gentle to a man. It gets under my skin at times. I could do with a sparring partner."

When John came up over the crest of the hill to where they sat, he saw his sister was laughing. He took in the sight hungrily, with great relief and joy in his face. William smiled and bent down to pick a flower of grass, which he twirled and picked to pieces in his fingers as Madeleine said, "This brother of yours has just committed a terrible indiscretion." It told her something about William and John's expectations of him that, despite her lighthearted and teasing tone, John immediately looked somewhat alarmed.

"What's he done?" he inquired gingerly.

"He has—without his abbot's permission, mind, Father John—invited me to leave this place and come live in a little cottage in St. Alcuin's close."

John's eyebrows shot up in surprise. Slowly, considering this, he came to sit with them on the grass. "Is that what you want?" he asked her.

"A little cottage with herbs and a place for hens, he said. With no rent. And I can browse a goat at the abbey. He said I will be safe because I am your sister, and I can come to chapel so people will not say I am a witch."

John said nothing. He bent his head, absently fingering the speedwell flowers in the grass, but gently, so as not to hurt the delicate petals.

"Adam? Would I be in the way?" Her voice sounded uncertain.

"No!" John shook his head with vehemence. "I mean, 'No, you would never be in the way,' not, 'No, you can't come.' I just feel so dreadfully ashamed I did not think to ask you myself, you and Mother both. What might I have avoided if—"

"Oh, for pity's sake, don't start that again!" William interrupted him. "I've heard enough self-flagellation from you to last me the rest of my life! Besides, you've only just been made abbot this last month. When did you have the authority to ask her before? Or when, I might add, did you have a cellarer with the wit to put the thought into your head? So can she come or not?"

Abbot John looked at Madeleine. "This is a fair sample of the insubordination and insufferable discourtesy I have daily to bear," he said. "My sweet sister, *of course* you can come. When? Now?"

"Father William said the cottage stands empty," she said, trying to conceal as best she could her eagerness. "I have nothing though. Everything is gone in the fire. I have no money to live on or to pay for furnishings."

"St. Alcuin's used to be a charitable house and kind," said John, "but we have this awful new cellarer's assistant now who counts every peppercorn and sends us out to pick the tarry wool that has caught on the thorns. I don't know if he will spare so much as a king's shilling for your upkeep."

"He's quite right." William looked at her with mock severity. "But you may thank heaven that their real cellarer, Brother Ambrose, is a more modest man, old and indulgent. He will give you enough to furnish the house, and spare half a dozen hens from our flock, *and* find you an allowance for your needs. His assistant might even feel emboldened to risk his disapproval by obtaining a dress for you to travel home in, so we don't get arrested for having kidnapped a Poor Clare. Or possibly two dresses, in case you turn out to have table manners like our Oswald. And, when I think about it, a woolen shawl and a warm cloak and a kerchief for Mass. Dear heaven, you're going to be expensive!"

"You—you are the cellarer's assistant?"

"I am. And Brother Thomas and Brother Stephen between them can make you a henhouse that will keep out Brother

Reynard when he does his nightly round. Do we have an agreement? Will I have added Mother Mary Beatrix to my list of enemies now?"

But the Reverend Mother understood. Getting into a monastic community was not usually easy: no superior stood in the way of a postulant who wanted to get out. Abbot John's proposition relieved the abbess of the predicament in which she found herself: wanting to help and shelter Madeleine without burdening the community with a sister whose vocation rested on spurious and inadequate foundations. Her almoner proved equally helpful, having only in the past week been given three bundles of discarded clothes to distribute to the poor. Two gowns—one green, one gray—were found to fit Madeleine; a winter cloak with a torn hem that wanted only a quiet evening to repair it; a knitted shawl of coarse cream Swaledale wool; some sturdy boots; and two kerchiefs to cover her head to drape for modesty or to keep out the chill.

Madeleine was offered no opportunity to make her farewells after John had said Mass on the following morning; it was not the custom. Her departure would be reported to Mother Mary Brigid who, as novice mistress, needed to know, but nobody else. Postulants came, and they went; every now and then somebody lasted the course. But Mother Mary Beatrix embraced her and blessed her; then with a squeeze of the hand and a promise to hold Madeleine fast in her prayers, the abbess left her waiting for Sister Mary Cuthbert to unlock the enclosure door.

As she stepped out of the monastery into the courtyard where William held their horses, while John made their gifts of money in thanks for the kind and generous hospitality shown them, Madeleine felt suddenly, wildly free. For an instant she could hardly catch her breath. As she quickly remembered her composure, she caught William's eye and saw him amused—and happy because she was happy. With a sense of exhilaration, she brought her pack for him to help her fasten it behind the saddle of John's old mare. There would always be scars and terrors of memory, but life could begin again.

"We'll have to wink at modesty, I fear, to get you home," William said. "You're as thin as a little bird; there's nothing of you, so the palfrey'll take you well enough riding up with Oswald. He's under strict instructions not to dribble down the back of your neck."

Then he asked her seriously: "Are you at ease with that, Madeleine? John and I meant to take turns to ride old Bess, but it's only twenty miles. He and I could both walk, and you could ride his mare with no companion if you'd rather."

Grateful at his concern for what she might need and feel, Madeleine thanked him with honest warmth. It was his sensitivity in giving her a choice that made the difference. She smiled at him, and as their eyes met she knew she had a friend.

CHAPTER
SIX

You two," said Brother Cormac with (as he pointed out to them quite forcibly) all charity and evangelical forbearance, "are nothing but gannets. You are the most horrible specimens of fallen humanity imaginable. Gluttony on legs, both of you! You make Brother Stephen's fattest sow look like a starved refugee in flight from Skellig Michael. Here am I, striving against all opposition to set an uplifting example to this overweight novice let loose on our kitchen with his fixation for pastry and fancy ways with a pigeon breast, and do you support my efforts to guide him into some kind of monastic abstinence and restraint? No. You hang around here at all times of the day like seagulls following the plow. What is it now?"

"We only wondered if you had some of those mushroom pasties left over from the midday meal," Father Francis began pitifully, "but if you think we'd be setting a bad example to Brother Conradus . . . "

" . . . we'd be willing to settle for your usual stodge—bread and honey or anything," Brother Tom hastily concluded, not liking the direction Father Francis seemed to be taking.

"You can't have the pasties. There are some, but our abbot's back, bringing an entourage with him, who will all have to be fed."

"John's back? Since when? Who's he brought? Ye saints and

little fishes! Why did no one think to tell me? I'd better take his pasties straight over and wait on his table!"

"It's not what you'd call a formal gathering, by all accounts." Cormac went to find the tray of pasties. "Oh, look—these two are a bit misshapen; I doubt they'd be missed. William de Bulmer has returned in one piece, avoiding suicide and every other attempt on his life. They have gathered up another stray monk, sans eyes and tongue and the Lord only knows what else. And Father John has brought his sister back to live in Peartree Cottage."

"Can I come too?" asked Francis as Brother Cormac stacked the tasty savories of Brother Conradus's making to be taken to the abbot's lodging. "I mean, that's a lot of pasties to carry on one platter. And no doubt they'll be wanting a jug of ale as well."

"Aye, and some of this apple cake; I think we'd best all go!"

So it was that their abbot, having made his way home not long before Vespers, taking it in turns with William to ride or walk while Madeleine rode with Oswald on William's gray palfrey, found his lodging besieged by a deputation of his brothers bearing refreshments and agog with curiosity.

"God bless you, brothers, we haven't even washed or barely set down our packs! By heaven, word travels fast in this house! My sister, Madeleine, I think you all know—she has been here many times to stay before. And this is Father Oswald, who will be part of this community. He's another delinquent reprobate of the house of St. Dunstan—what did you say, William? You wager I can't spell that? I certainly can! But he, as I was saying before I was so rudely interrupted, though undeniably depraved is not a patch on his prior when it comes to rank villainy. And we've weathered *him*; so Father Oswald should fit right in. Sadly, he cannot eat these delectable tidbits you've brought us because they'd choke him. Brother Cormac, Father Francis, if you would take him across to the kitchen and find him some soup or some bread and milk, that would be better.

He'll need an apron or a cloth, if you'll kindly provide one. He has no tongue, and that makes it tricky to eat. I would come with you, but I have one more task to attend to before the light fades or the Vespers bell starts to ring. Father Oswald, these are your new brothers: Father Francis, currently helping in the guest house; Brother Thomas, who is my esquire; Brother Cormac, who keeps our pastry chef under control in the kitchen."

Oswald stood and, with all senses alert, took into both his hands first Francis's warm dry, gentle hand, then Tom's brawny hand with the rough knuckles and callused palm, then Cormac's long, bony hand.

"He cannot see and though he can speak to you, at first you're not likely to get what he's saying," remarked William. "But he is not deaf, and what wits he ever had are still intact: so nobody will need to speak to him loudly and slowly."

Francis laughed. "Will you come with us then to the kitchen, Father Oswald? You'll be hungry after your journey, and it seems unfair to have you standing by while these three wolf down all those pasties."

"Oh—" added William as Oswald put out his hand to be led away, "when you walk with a blind man, you should let *him* take *your* arm, and you lead him. If *you* take *his* arm and steer him, he being unable to see where to go, you make him too vulnerable, in reality as well as in how he feels. If you let *him* take *your* arm instead, he will feel more secure and you will progress more effectively. Isn't that right, Mistress Hazell?"

Madeleine nodded emphatically, her eyes full of laughter. "'Tis exactly so," she said, watching with approval as Cormac held the door open and Oswald passed through with confidence, having taken Francis's arm.

"So," said Abbot John, "I know you are itching to see Peartree Cottage, Madeleine. There is just time to go and take a quick look before Vespers. Will you come with us, Brother

Thomas? William thinks there may be some small repairs to be done, and you'll be our handiest man for that."

"You three go ahead—you can see the garden anyway—while I run across to the checker and fetch the key," William said. "I'll be with you in no time."

The close came within the boundary of the outer wall, itself bounded with a low wall separating it from the greensward around the church. Madeleine saw at once she would be safe there: no one could come to the close without entering through the great gates at the porter's permission. Because they were enclosed in this way, the gardens as well as the houses were small, and they were few. Those who had bought corrodies lived in them, and someone had recently died. Peartree Cottage, as its name suggested, had an ancient fruit tree, its bark silver-lichened, its twigs and branches gnarled and twisty, growing at the front.

"Yes, this gate needs repair, which is what William said," John remarked. They examined it together.

"The hinge has rusted; the wood isn't rotten. That's easily repaired," said Brother Tom.

"He also volunteered you to make a henhouse."

"Did he so? Father William is making very free with my time!" But Tom did not look as though he minded.

Madeleine had slipped into the little garden at the front and was examining its plants with delight. "We have a whole pharmacy here!" she exclaimed. "Somebody knew what they were doing!"

From the checker William came walking, his light, swift step only slightly wearied by their trek home. "Your key, good madam. Will you let us in?" He gave it into her hand, and, excited, she unlocked the house.

The low doorway with its pointed arch gave directly into the main room of the cottage. The substantial fireplace had been swept clean of ashes, but the cooking irons still hung from their nails on the walls, the pot was still hanging from its chain. A table and two stools were there and, on the board, two pewter plates, two wooden bowls, two earthenware beakers of Brother Thaddeus's making, a candlestick with a candle half-burned still in it, a knife, and a handful of spoons—some wood, some horn. "That candle is beeswax, not tallow," said Madeleine contentedly.

A ladder staircase led up out of this room, and Madeleine climbed it into the bedroom, where a wooden bedstead stood against the chimney wall, with no mattress, but a blanket folded neatly on its boards. A wooden chest stood under the little window and a chamber pot under the bed. "This is perfect . . . perfect!" she whispered.

"If you go to the infirmary in the morning, Brother Michael will help you make a mattress," John said.

They went carefully down the narrow staircase, and Madeleine unlatched the door at the back of the room. It led into a small scullery, where a stone floor and a capacious stone sink, with a wooden pail and an earthenware pitcher left in it, provided a place for washing. From there a door opened into the garden behind the cottage, where two apple trees grew, and a profusion of herbs.

"The henhouse could go right there!" Madeleine whipped around, her eyes alight, for Brother Tom's agreement. "At your service, my lady," he said.

"Friends, by the light I think the Vespers bell will soon be rung," said Abbot John after he felt the garden had been adequately inspected. "Madeleine, we can come again tomorrow. You can keep the key anyway."

They trooped back into the cottage, and Brother Tom went through to the front to check again what he would need for the gate. John crossed the room to the fireplace to look up the chimney. "I did have it swept!" said William instantly.

"This is so timely," John said. Turning back to them, his face happy, he was almost knocked off his feet by his sister's sudden embrace. "Thank you, my brother, thank you, thank you!" She hugged him tight as he held her close to him. "My sister, my dear little sister," he murmured. "I love you so much."

William had turned his back on this scene of family tenderness and was counting the spoons on the table and checking that the drinking vessels were not cracked or chipped when he felt a tap on his shoulder. "This was your idea, Brother." He turned and found himself looking into her eyes, shining with happiness. "God reward you! God reward you!" As she suddenly, shyly hugged him and released him again, he laughed, saying, "Yes, I think he just did!"

"And you will feel safe here—even sleeping alone?" John asked.

"It's a tight little cottage, all of stone and no thatch. I have a key. It's walled at the back, and the abbey gates are shut at night. What's to be afraid of? Thank you, my brother. I shall be safe here. And now there's your Vespers bell."

"Stay in the guest house tonight, and we will make you comfortable in your cottage tomorrow," said John as they walked from the close the short distance to the church.

"Adam, how will I ever repay this?"

"You don't have to even think—"

"She most certainly does!" cut in William. "With your permission, Father Abbot! If you can be of assistance to Brother Walafrid, we shall be grateful, Madeleine—especially if you can make a better bottle of wine than his present weird concoctions. You have already made an elegant job of sewing Oswald's eyes, which none of us could do, so for a start I think this is us repaying you. A surgeon's fees are not cheap. Another midwife is always welcome for the village also, and that's obviously not something we offer at present—well, only for the ewes. I understand you can keep accounts. I sorely need some help, especially around Lady Day and Michaelmas when we get the rents in.

We shall work your fingers to the bone. We shall keep you up late and get you up early. Think you not for a moment this cottage comes unearned, for it does not! There is more work to put your hand to than you can possibly imagine. I don't know how we did without you!"

They parted from Madeleine in the nave of the church where a few devout villagers sat in the benches here and there. Tom walked ahead into the choir, but William paused, bending his head close to hear his abbot's quiet words as the two of them went around the parish altar into the choir together. "My friend, you are a genius. What a kind touch of healing that was. God bless you. I owe you so much." "Nay, idiot; I owe you my life," William's reply was audible only to John as he left his abbot's side to take his seat in his stall.

As he sat down, he saw John had paused and was looking at him. He recognized in a flash that the word *idiot* would not do, however affectionately meant. John had become his friend, but he was his abbot first.

In a discreet gesture he smote his breast. "*Mea culpa*," he murmured respectfully, and his abbot nodded and walked on to his stall.

The whole community could see that their abbot had returned to them in a different frame of mind. They observed him at Vespers and at Compline, and they saw he had found peace. A sense of well-being and relief spread through them all. Without question they had loved him and upheld him in the extremity of his grief; but when the leader of a community loses hope and courage, the ripples spread to the edges and back again. The bleeding away of vitality does not confine itself to the man. A lightness traveled through the common life that suppertime as the brothers rejoiced that their abbot had come home to them whole again.

On the following morning, the eve of Pentecost, Father Chad read to them the chapter of the day—a portion of a long chapter spread over four days, on the tools of the spiritual craft.

Father Chad picked up where the reader of the day before had left off, reminding the brothers that they must be faithful in obeying every day what God had laid upon them: loving holy chastity, never indulging in hatred of anybody at all, never allowing bitterness to take root in their souls, not giving way to jealousy or entertaining themselves by picking fights with each other. They were to run away from any conceitedness and smug pride, treat the senior monks with profound respect and be gentle with the young ones. They were to pray especially for those who disliked them or with whom they never could get on. If any quarrel did arise between them, both the Rule and the Bible laid down that they must not let the sun set without making their peace. And they should never, ever despair of God's mercy.

Abbot and brothers together heard these wise and kind words, letting the generosity and goodness of Benedict's way feed their hearts and sink into their souls. The silence of reflection lengthened as they meditated on all they had heard. And then they turned their attention to what their abbot had to say.

John spoke to them with his characteristic straightforward humility.

"I'm sorry, this isn't a proper homily—I've been thinking so hard about what I want to say to you that I hadn't even read today's chapter very carefully to think of any comment I could make upon it, though it is beautiful.

"I don't know if this is news or teaching or what it is: I'm just telling you about a time when I've seen the Gospel meet real life. Friends, tomorrow is Pentecost. Today is the last day in Ascensiontide. My thanks to Father Chad for his pastoral care of you while I have been away.

"So we achieved what we set out to do. We found Father

Oswald and brought him home. You will all have met him by now.

"When I spoke to you last, all of us gathered together like this, it was the day before Ascension Day. Less than two weeks have passed since then, but so much has changed. I know you have held us—me—steadily in your prayers, and I am more grateful than I can express to you. What has happened has been a kind of miracle, and though I've been thinking so hard about how to explain it to you, I'm still not sure I have the words for what I want to say.

"I don't delude myself that you hang onto every word I impart to you in Chapter here, but I think maybe you might remember what I said to you before I went away. I was devastated by what happened to my sister. Everything seemed to be shattered and blown to pieces. When I went to see her, she could barely look at me. I was shredded inside by the sense of guilt that my family had been attacked with no one to protect and shield them. I could not bear human company. Nor could she. Father William came with me to Chesterfield, to search for Oswald. You know well what Father William's trials have been; he has felt lonely and isolated from human society. He is the first to say he brought his trouble on his own head, but be that as it may, he has felt frightened and alone, and for many a year before all this his faith meant little to him and human company even less.

"Three people, all entirely involved in their own troubles, tormented by their own demons, eaten up with guilt and shame and fear, wanting neither to touch nor be touched, but just to be left alone to heal after all that had happened.

"We'd all three of us got to the pupation stage, I guess. We had come through what life had handed out to us, deservedly or not, but were each in a strange hermit's cell of shock, coming to terms with what had happened and who and what that made us now.

"Then we met Father Oswald, and suddenly everything changed, because he needed our help. Down on my knees in the street at his side, trying to see in the half-light of the alleyway just what cruelty had been worked on him, I forgot about myself and that I couldn't bear anyone to touch me. He's blind. He needed someone to hold his hand. In similar wise, Father William had to get over himself and his aversion for all things human because Father Oswald needed his help to eat and manage even the basics of life. So we came to Motherwell, where my sister, Madeleine, had taken refuge with the Poor Clares. Cold and remote in shock and hurt, she remained reluctant to meet us—until she saw Father Oswald. She could not bear to greet me with any kind of contact, but she came to the grille to touch Oswald's face, to look with care at what he needed to have done. She is skilled in the healing arts, and she sutured his eyes for him, which I was nervous of doing.

"Do you remember I said to you, before we went away, that one day I would find my way to the Father and be able to bear the vulnerability of human touch again?

"Now this is where words begin to fail me—when I try to explain the grace I have glimpsed. Please make the best you can of my stumbling offering. God is all compassion. God, three in one, is community in love. God is creator, who goes on making us and remaking us even when our hearts are broken and our lives shattered. He searches for every shard of who we once were and makes something new of all those pieces and his love.

"It was when we—me, Madeleine, William—forgot ourselves, and our hearts were drawn beyond our own troubles into compassion for someone else, that healing began for each of us. It was when we worked together and drew into a common way that cheerfulness began again: laughter and fresh courage and the reassurance that we were forgiven and no longer alone. Out of the hopelessness came a new beginning. From the black tomb to the cold air of the uncertain light of dawn. Then from that frozen beginning to an ascent into the Father heart of God.

"We have come home different—I mean different because we were hurt as well as because we were healed. Madeleine, William, I—our souls are a bit scarred and knocked about, and we are more vulnerable now. But that's not a bad thing; woundedness can be a source of compassion, like the sweet water springs that breach the intactness of the earth. And we owe so much—so very much—to Father Oswald, for finding us where we were hurt and bringing us home."

When John had finished speaking, and the day's news and novices' confessions were shared, the young men of the novitiate rose to leave. They closed the door behind them with anxious care, Brother Benedict, last out, achieving a good result with only a sharp click of the latch to indicate they had gone. Their novice master would follow them at the conclusion of Chapter; for now they went ahead of him up the day stairs to the novitiate, where they took their places in the teaching circle of assorted stools and short benches. This was really supposed to be a time of reflective silence, and sometimes it was. They seated themselves quietly and without fuss, as they had been taught, but then Brother Cassian said, "I can hardly believe the cruelty of all that they did to him."

The faint stir among the group affirmed this as their common mind and the focus of their thoughts.

"Father Oswald?" said Conradus (he thought he'd better check).

"Brother Michael says we have to be really careful of what we give him to eat." Conscious of the extra status his work in the infirmary conferred upon him, Brother Benedict enjoyed the immediate attention of his seven fellow novices. "I never thought about it before, but of course you can't swallow without a tongue; that's why he dribbles all the time. And because he can't swallow properly, he just has to poke things down his throat or kind of toss them back. Brother Michael says there's a huge chance of the food going down the wrong way and choking him—to death even! And even if it doesn't choke him, it could get right down into his chest and give him pneumonia, like Father William."

Brother Robert laughed. "'Pneumonia' is quite a good description of Father William—kind of pale and thin with scary eyes."

"What? No—I meant—"

"Yes, yes, we know what you meant. Is that how Father William got pneumonia then? Choked on his food?"

Brother Benedict stopped, aware he had committed an indiscretion. The world of the novices was kept very separate from the life of the professed brothers, but the infirmary work gave glimpses into everybody's secrets. "No," he said.

Brother Robert looked puzzled. "But you just said—"

"Forget what I just said! I shouldn't have. He . . . no. No, I mustn't say. Anyway we have to be very watchful for Father Oswald and hit him hard on the back if he goes purple or looks like he's choking. It's hard to tell, actually, because sometimes his food starts to go down the wrong way, and then he has to hawk it back up again for another try. Hawking or choking; choking or hawking—it's a bit tense, especially when it might be a matter of life and death. It'll be every meal too!"

The young men pondered this soberly.

"Father John's sister sewed his eyes up for him," continued Brother Benedict, reveling in his role as a mine of information this May morning. "She can do surgery and deliver babies and read and write as good as a priest, apparently. She's come to live here. I don't know why. Perhaps they need her to help look after Father Oswald. Perhaps she was afraid to live alone after she was set upon."

They heard the footfall of their novice master on the stairs, and conversation ceased.

CHAPTER SIX

✠   ✠   ✠

Brother Thomas built Madeleine a henhouse and repaired her gate. William brought her two sheepskins from the store they kept to sell. He fetched her all the provisions she needed to create a home and larder, and she grew to know the sound of his approaching footsteps.

Quite often, as evening fell and the day's work in the checker was done, instead of making his way directly to the cloister for Vespers, William would cross the abbey court in the other direction toward the close and make sure that all was well in Peartree Cottage.

He brought her firewood and linen sheets. "I'm sorry—just now we can only spare two. Can you manage with that? That should see you through the summer; you can wash them and dry them in a day in this weather."

Most of all, he brought her friendship. His wit struck sparks from hers, and she liked to see his blue-green eyes alight with laughter and his thin face break into the merriment of his smile.

"William never smiles, not really. I don't know what you've done to him!" said Brother Tom.

And she laughed. "Oh . . . well, he smiles at me," she said.

Brother Tom commented on this with astonishment to Father John as he cleared the ashes from the hearth for the last time now that the evenings could be counted warm enough even for the comfort of guests. "I didn't know that man *could* smile! No wonder they thought she was a witch! Then again, maybe it's a miracle—it's so hard to tell!"

He carried on sweeping, unaware he had made any particular impression. But his abbot had stopped what he was doing and was listening to him with greater attention than Tom would have expected.

Spring moved into summer, and the elderflowers hung

heavy on the trees. The lime flowers gave out their beautiful fragrance, the hay stood almost ready for mowing, and the fine days took on a languor of heat as the weather held dry.

Abbot John came through the wooden gate in the wall, which Brother Thomas had fixed. Finding the door ajar, he went into the cottage to look for Madeleine. Hearing voices from outside at the back, he continued into the scullery, where the door to the garden stood open. Outside he saw his sister reprimanding his cellarer's assistant in no uncertain terms. He stopped just within the doorway and stood quietly to watch this exchange.

"No, good brother, that is *not* a weed! I turn my back five minutes, and you take out some of the best herbs in my garden! Why didn't you pay attention to what I told you? Put it back!"

John noticed with a certain astonishment that William looked distinctly chastened.

"Will it grow again all right even though I pulled it up?"

"Grow? Of course it'll grow! It's a plant! William, have you never done any gardening before in all your life?"

"You know . . . " The sun was in William's eyes, but he squinted in her direction anyway. ". . . they will never burn you for a witch in these parts, but I have little evidence to stand in the way of their ducking you in the village pond for a scold!"

"Aye, but they'll change their tune when they find out who was on the receiving end of the scolding, think you not? To work, monk! *Labore est orare!*"

"A shred of respect and a cup of ale wouldn't go amiss, sweet madam. Oh, God bless us, here's my abbot. Is it to defend me or am I to be harried now from every side?"

John came out into the garden and walked between the herb beds and under the apple trees to where they stood.

"I'm relieved to see that Father William is capable of getting his hands dirty on occasion," he said. "But there are some matters awaiting his attention. Brother Ambrose is feeling badly neglected. He's just been holding forth to me at some length about the grading and storing of the fleeces that are coming off the shearing. He says they need sorting, and lanolin brings him out in a rash. He wants to know if he's to ask Brother Thomas to clean the ditches around the top meadow or if you engaged somebody from the village, and if so, whom? He's lost the bill for the cruets you ordered for the refectory. Do you know where it is? I think he said they would cost nine shillings and four pence, and I hope that's not true. He's also talking to me about one Samuel Walton, rope maker, concerning cords for girths and cords for tethering the horses out in the pasture. He also has things to say about how many ambras of white salt and lump salt we may require. Oh, and he wonders if you intended a hundred and fifty horseshoes or only a hundred, and in consequence, how many nails? I'm impressed at myself remembering that complex shopping list, so I hope you are too; but I'll be heartily glad if you can come and attend to the business yourself. To set Father William to work pulling weeds is not playing to his strengths, my sister, and I think you might be equal to the task yourself. Is all well with the cottage and the garden? Did Brother Stephen bring you a sheepskin for your bed? Bless you then. I'll be seeing you anon. Father William, I'll walk over with you."

The two men went back through the cottage, Madeleine waving a cheery farewell as they left her among the garden herbs, preparing to take some cuttings from the rosemary and the pinks.

"One word only," said John gently as he closed the cottage gate behind them. "Boundaries."

They walked to the end of the close in silence. "She needs a little help to settle in," said William in casual tone. "She has some ghosts to lay to rest but seems to me to be doing well." He shrugged, easy, imperturbable. "Still, she'll do just fine by herself now for sure."

John walked slowly, and William suited his pace to his abbot's.

"William," John said, "you're falling in love with my sister, and throwing dust in my eyes is not going to work. Your place here is precarious, but hers is even more so. You put one foot across that boundary and you put her home at risk for sure, and possibly yours as well. You can't afford to do this. The path you're treading is ill-advised. You have to let this go."

He stopped. "Are you hearing me?"

"She is in need of friendship."

They walked on.

"She's in need of *our* friendship, not *your* friendship."

"How does that work then? We are but people, individuals. It's not possible, surely, to be a friend to someone without spending time with her."

John shook his head. "She must make her own friends among the folk she finds here—layfolk, not the monks—where are you going?"

"To the checker—that way. You told me to sort out the purchases with Brother Ambrose."

"Oh, never mind Ambrose! He can wait five minutes to find out about his cords and his ambras of salt. You're coming with me because this is important."

They continued in silence toward the principal buildings of the abbey, the abbot's lodge opening onto the court as well as the cloister. Just before they reached the door, they were hailed from behind. "Ah, Father William! I've been looking for you all over!"

They both turned to respond, and William looked at his abbot as Brother Ambrose stooped momentarily, his hands to his knees, out of breath.

John shook his head no, just the slightest movement, and William waited without speaking.

"Better?" said Abbot John in a friendly, genial tone as

Ambrose righted himself. "I have apprised Father William of the things he must attend to, and he will be with you presently," he continued before Ambrose could say anything. "Do not fret. He knows and will give this his proper attention within the hour. I'm sorry, Ambrose—I've kept him busy with other things, but he will be all yours in a little while."

Brother Ambrose nodded, still puffing. "That's all I needed to know."

William still said nothing. Ambrose turned back for the checker, and John opened the door to his lodge. They entered to find Brother Thomas sweeping the floor. "Thanks, friend!" said John cheerfully. "That looks better, but can I ask you to set the task aside for a brief while? I have to speak with William."

Brother Tom swept the dust he had gathered to the edge of the room and propped the broom against the wall, standing with its bristles on the dust to keep that anchored. He moved obediently toward the cloister door, and John caught the expression on his face. He saw that Tom was beginning to feel hurt by the intimacy he perceived between his abbot and William.

"Sit down, William," said John. "Wait a minute."

He followed Brother Thomas, stopping the door with his hand as Tom began to pull it shut. Tom looked back in surprise. "Brother, tonight I still have no one to dine with me and intended to do as I told you and eat in the frater. But why don't you come and eat supper with me? I think I've seen less of you since you've been my esquire than in all the years we've been together in community."

John felt relieved to see the warmth in Tom's eyes. "Aye, gladly. I have to finish off a repair to a worm-eaten chest I started yesterday for Theodore, so I'll go and do that while you're busy now. I'll come back and clean up here once it's properly fixed, if that suits you."

With a smile and a nod of thanks, John closed the door behind him. "Where were we?" he said.

"I believe you were in the middle of telling me that I am falling in love with your sister and ought to keep out of her way."

"Don't go frosty on me, William; that's a power game. Are you telling me I'm wrong?" John found it hard, always, to hold the gaze of those pale eyes regarding him thoughtfully, but he did. In the end it was William who looked away. "No, I'm not."

John sat examining this ambiguous reply, suspecting that he had been offered it as a dodge to secure time. He decided that if time was what William needed, he could have it. So he said nothing.

"Oh—I'm sorry!" said William, suddenly realizing John thought he was being evasive. "I meant, 'no, I'm not telling you you're wrong,' not, 'no, I don't care for Madeleine.'"

John took this in. He knew it was true, but at the same time he almost wished it had not been said. Naming anything brings it one step further into manifest reality.

"I guess this is part of why I never thought to invite Madeleine and my mother here before," mused John. "Women and monastic communities of men can be a fair disastrous combination. We have enough trouble with Our Lady of Sorrows in the chapel. Women guests fall in love with the monks, or the monks fall in love with them, and either way there's trouble."

"Give me credit for a little discretion, Father John!"

"On the basis of what? If it's plain to me you're getting more close to Madeleine than you should be, do you think it won't be noticeable to anyone else?"

"Madeleine won't see," said William quietly.

"Won't she? What makes you think so?"

"Because . . . because of the way my head thinks," William answered him slowly.

"Whatever's that supposed to mean?"

"Whatever emotions I might feel, however deep or strong they may be, there is always a dispassionate watcher in my head, evaluating, noticing, commenting. I never lose myself totally to anything. It can be quite wearisome sometimes—an endless internal critique of all I say and do. And I know—oh, now I'm going to have to be honest with you, and that isn't easy to do either, so please don't be angry with me—I know that Madeline will never see that I . . . what I feel.

"I know she will not see because at the level of my being that feels—my emotional self, my heart—I myself cannot properly see what *she* feels about *me*. On that level of my being, unless I could . . . oh, unless I could hold her in my arms and have her as my own—which, don't you worry, I'm not even dreaming of . . . well, that is to say, yes, I *am* dreaming of it, but I have no intention of doing any such thing. But unless I could do that, my heart would never really know for sure what she feels about me, because I want it so much I can't believe it could be true.

"That's my heart. But my head, watching and commenting, deduces dispassionately that one of two things must be true. Either she does not care for me as I do for her—or else she does.

"And my head knows that a woman who has not long since been raped, not once but repeatedly, is bound to feel nervous around men. If she had even a whiff of a notion of what I feel for her and did not reciprocate it, then she would find it threatening to be with me by herself.

"On the other hand, if she is drawn to me as I am to her, I know that—just like me—without the confirmation, the assurance that comes with the embrace of love, she would never quite let herself believe that I care for her because she too much wants it to be true.

"So since she is not nervous in my company and finds me not the slightest bit threatening, I have deduced that what I feel for her is indeed reciprocated, but it is channeled into friendly banter, where I think it's safe."

John was listening to this analysis with a certain expression of amazement.

"Safe? God save and help us! You think what you have just told me represents anything that could be called *safe*? William, you have been the superior of a community! Put yourself in my shoes! If you had just had this conversation, would you be blithely describing such a relationship as *safe*?"

The faintest smile moved William's mouth. "I think you have never grasped quite what our community was like, Father John. What the men did with each other, and what they did with the maids, never interested me. I focused my attention on what they did with the money. In fact, I have wondered if there was something of retribution for this in the attack Oswald suffered. I meant it when I told you he was no angel. So long as they kept themselves on the right side of the undergarments of the aristocracy, I didn't intervene overmuch or attempt to curtail the activities of the men of my house."

John had no answer for this. "Oh, dear." William sighed. "You look appalled."

"Yes, I think I am. So living a double life is something you're used to?"

"No. Not personally. At least not in this respect. I think I've said to you before, I do not—normally—like closeness. I do not attach. Human relationship feels somewhat imprisoning to me. I have not been pure, sexually, but I have been solitary."

Their eyes met. "Thank God you are honest at least," said John, "but, William, this with Madeleine has got to stop—not slow down or rein in a little: *stop*."

William's face betrayed no emotion beyond the flicker of his eyes that John had come to recognize as the sign that all was far from well.

"That will be hard on her," he replied softly after thinking on John's words for a short while. "She is very vulnerable. She has no friends here."

"Exactly. She is *completely* vulnerable. And she never will make friends if this continues; all she will make is scandal, because what I have seen, others will see too. The way you look at her, the way you make her laugh, the way she is so free in how she speaks to you and you to her . . . there is no distance, there is no caution. Are you telling me you cannot see this?"

Reluctantly William shook his head. "I can see it perfectly well," he admitted, "but I'd been telling myself it would be all right—I could manage it with grace, let it run its course and die, so neither Madeleine nor anyone else would ever know."

"Monastic celibacy is such a balancing act," said John more gently. "It's nigh impossible to keep your heart open and humanly tender, but still keep a guard on your relationships with others so that warmth does not slide into an exclusive intimacy of one kind or another. For apart from this disastrous friendship with Madeleine, you are too close to me as well, in some ways. Too familiar."

As he said that, it was as though a painful remoteness closed around William, who leaned forward on his stool, his elbows on his knees, the lower part of his face resting on his hands. He moved his head slightly, rubbing his mouth thoughtfully against his hand. Then he was just still. John realized that despite his perceptiveness and subtle intelligence, when it came to personal relationships, William was in effect still a novice. He had simply ignored that whole territory for most of his life. John felt the struggle and the sadness in his brother; the familiar healer's stab of sharp compassion passed like a blade through his gut.

William sat up straight to look at him. "It is Christ who has done this," he said. "He broke me open. He has made me vulnerable. It is too painful, John, and I'm not used to it. What can I do? What will be my refuge now? Without you, without Madeleine—" He shook his head, the words tailing into silence again.

"Do you want an answer to that?" John asked gently.

"Yes, I do!" In a sudden, convulsive movement William clutched both hands to his own belly, as if it hurt him badly. "Ah! It feels so . . . ah!"

John waited, watching the agonized restlessness as William tried to become reconciled to this new perspective.

"I was supposed to do this years ago, wasn't I? Not in middle life. This belongs to the novitiate! Well, I feel suitably foolish and embarrassed. I might have hoped by midlife I should have found the dignity of some stability—which I had before Christ broke me open."

"A hard shell is not the same thing as dignity," John said quietly. "The only constructive way to deal with this is simply to take the love and share it out. Notice it, feel it, and give it away. The love that wants to pour out to Madeleine—and, God bless you, to me—give some to Ambrose, give some to Tom, to Germanus, to Francis, to Father Chad."

At that William suddenly laughed. "I was doing all right until you mentioned Father Chad! Lord, have mercy! Does *anyone* love Chad?"

"If they don't," replied his abbot, "isn't it time somebody did?"

"Leave that one alone for a minute," said William. "This is difficult enough. Please don't bring Father Chad into the mix. Can I be clear about something? Are you asking me *not to see* Madeleine? To avoid her?"

"I am."

"Won't that hurt her? Won't she feel snubbed and rejected?"

"Yes."

William looked at him, bewildered.

"If she does," said his abbot gently, "she will conclude she was mistaken—that you were only being kind, to help her settle in, and we will be able to retrieve a more appropriate balance of relationship. She will be glad she made no real indiscretion and hope you did not see how she felt for you. She will look for friends among the villagers who come to her for help. She will find the community is her friend and will watch over her and not let her be lonely. You must do this, for I tell you, William, you are playing with fire. Let things, as they are, go one step further and you will have her in your arms; then she will end up having to be placed in a women's community, while you look for employment with a merchant of some kind in York. Such emotions are too powerful, too elemental, to both contain and feed at the same time. You will soon be subsisting from day to day on the minutes you can snatch with her. Oh God, help us—you already are, aren't you? I can see it in your face!"

John watched the struggle inside his friend, understood the wrenching depth of the sacrifice he needed to make. It happened to so many men, and it never was easy.

In the end, "I will do this," said William simply. "I will give up both of you. I have made particular friendships, and it is not my right to do so. But . . . look, I'm speaking to you now as my abbot: I want you to know—for no one else will know it, I shall not let them see—for the rest of my life, I shall keep John and I shall keep Madeleine in a shining memory of summer in my heart. I can let the relationships go, the day-to-day delight of friendship that has so sweetened my life, because I want to stay here. But before God, I cannot let her go—or you go—from my heart. You will be sewn into the beating of my heart with invisible thread, both of you. I promise you though, I swear it, nobody will see. I have lied all my life. I can lie about this. Will that do? Ah, merciful Jesu, Father! Don't look at me like that! Will you have me in tears? I can do no more!"

"William, let it settle. I am still here, and yes, there are bonds between us that shall not be forgotten or denied. Madeleine is here. And because of your initiative she is safe and not shut inside a convent where she does not belong. Being in love—it subsides; no, trust me, it does! You will not always feel as wretched as you are feeling this minute. And you will always be the man who helped her live again. She knows you are a monk. She will understand. She might feel hurt at first when you do not come to her, but that of itself will create a cooling space most necessary. Brother, our Father Peregrine said to Brother Thomas one time that love has no defenses, that you only know it's love when it hurts. I think about that sometimes. If we make the choice to stay alive—vital and tender and open—we've chosen something that is precious and therefore costly. If I've understood it rightly, what Christ asks of us is to accept the pain of being open. That's the picture of the cross—the pain of being open."

William nodded. "And this is you, my lord abbot, hammering the nails in?"

John swallowed. "I think it probably is," he said.

"It's a rhythm, isn't it?" said William slowly. "Crucifixion . . . burial . . . resurrection . . . ascension. You think you're through, you rejoice that it's done, and then before you know it, it starts again with a fresh crucifixion. Oh holy Jesus, I don't know that I have the strength for this."

"It *is* painful, but it doesn't rot you from the inside, like living for yourself and for material things and being shut away. It asks a great deal, but your brothers understand. Brother Tom, for instance—he has been in love. He was out of the community for quite some time, but he came back; he chose what he really wanted. Take the treasure that is in you and give it to the people who don't have any—Father Chad, Father Gilbert, the novices who are so unsure of themselves and desperate for affirmation, the merchants and traders who notice how coming here makes them feel."

William took these ideas in, considering what had been said to him, his face thoughtful. Then he seemed to come to a resolution; and when he spoke, his voice sounded wooden—the flat tone of resignation. "I'm taking up your time."

"If you love me, pray for me; and I will pray for you," said John gently, "for I love you too."

William nodded and got to his feet. "I'd best go and get the cords and the salt sorted out," he said.

John also stood, and they crossed the room to the door that led out to the cloister. William hesitated then and looked at his abbot. "She's . . . she's scared of big spiders," he said.

"Oh, for heaven's sake!" John stared at him in exasperation. "You are *not* to go near her! Anyway, I know about the spiders. She's my sister. But she's forty-three; that's grownup enough to come to terms with spiders."

William opened the door, but with his hand on the latch he looked back. "May I just—"

"Absolutely not," said John. "Leave her alone. Get on with the work you are supposed to be doing."

Nothing in his abbot's demeanor let William know that it broke John's heart to see the look on his friend's face as he nodded one more time and turned to go.

✠   ✠   ✠

As the days expanded into high summer, England stood green beneath her canopy of trees. In Madeleine's garden, the sound of contented hens against the drowsy hum of bees told the season, with the fragrance of the flowers.

A steady trickle of visitors began to find their way to Peartree Cottage as word quickly reached the village that she was a wisewoman skilled in herbal lore and practice, and an experienced midwife too. One or two women in the village were with child, and the walk up to the abbey was steep but not very far. Brother Michael respected Madeleine's knowledge and experience, and working alongside him she was able to contribute much of value to the medical help St. Alcuin's could offer the folk round about. Under the shelter of the abbey's good name and intrinsic holiness, Madeleine found herself able to interact freely and with confidence; she started to make friends. John came when he could spare an hour to spend in her company and invited her often to eat at his table and meet those who came and went.

Oswald learned the way to her house and frequently went to see her. Brother Michael visited from time to time to seek her advice.

The brothers saw that she lacked nothing. She had the eggs from her hens and the herbs from her garden, and Brother Ambrose brought her flour and oil, candles and spices, needles and thread, a spindle for the wool she collected from the hedgerows, and everything she needed.

She loved her cottage and lived contentedly there, but she commented with elaborate carelessness to her brother one June day, "It's odd, I never see William anymore."

"No? He says he's found you a goat. He was asking after you."

"A goat? Oh, God bless him!" Madeleine exclaimed, delighted. "I miss him though," she persisted tentatively.

"Yes, I understand. We keep him busy with his cellarer's duties, Madeleine. When we traveled together to Chesterfield, I think they felt his absence more sorely here than mine! His responsibilities are both broad and detailed; they leave him little leisure. No doubt your paths will cross from time to time."

Familiar with the nuances of John's voice, Madeleine knew she was hearing something that rang not quite true. She looked at him, puzzled. Very straight, he met her eyes. "Leave it, please, sister," he said. And then she understood.

In the checker each day, William worked diligently alongside Brother Ambrose. "I don't know how we ever got on without him," that brother remarked to his abbot one evening in late June as he fell into step with him on the way to Vespers. "For a week or two after you came back from Chesterfield, I hardly saw him, and I thought he was going to turn out to have been another nine days' wonder like Brother Bernard was when Father Peregrine tried him on the job—such promise but coming to nothing in the end. It takes stamina to keep at the cellarer's duties. Still, I expect Father William was busy helping Father Oswald find his way about that week or two, poor soul."

"I expect that must have been it," his abbot replied. "I'm pleased to hear he's settled back in again now."

As June turned into July, John asked William to bring to the abbot's lodge the last month's accounts to be approved and signed.

Finding his abbot seated at his great oak table, William handed him the bundle of prepared accounts. They had seen little of each other in the weeks since William had undertaken to sever all communication with Madeleine and to allow greater space between himself and his abbot. They saw each other in the daily round of worship, of course, and their paths crossed often enough as they each went about their business in the abbey. But the intimacy that had grown between them had been left on ice.

As William came into the room now, John appraised him carefully: the narrow, sallow, mobile face, with the silver hair and eyes the indeterminate cold color of the ocean—eyes whose color it was hard to remember and, like the sea, showing only the shifting surface, all manner of life without explanation continuing unobserved underneath. William's manner was pleasant and courteous. He gave no signal of special relationship; nothing in his glance or his demeanor suggested intimacy or friendship beyond their formal relationship in community. This man was hard to read.

Abbot John went through the accounts while William stood quietly waiting. He checked everything carefully, signing his name to each section and to all the letters ready for sending.

"Well?" As he pushed the bulky pile of parchments, duly examined and authorized, across the table, he looked into his friend's eyes with gentle concern. He probed with healer's sight, gazing directly into William's eyes, searching his soul, and saw . . . nothing. William's soul was not available for inspection. "Your head's in good form. How's your heart?"

Relaxing his guard somewhat, William shook his head, looking all of his fifty years. "I don't know that you should ask or that I should tell you," he said at last. He glanced at John and away again. "Sometimes when I have lain awake in the hot dark these summer nights, I have pressed my mouth to my own hand, pretending it was her I kissed. Sometimes as I could not sleep, I have wrapped my own arms around myself, pretending she held me close. I will spare you the graphic details of anything else I may have done. But I promise you I have never gone near her—not once, Father."

He picked up the bundle of documents and held them with both arms against himself as though they afforded some kind of protection. "Will that be all, Father?" His voice carefully neutral and light, he stood poised to go, waiting to be dismissed.

John's eyes met his. "'William—" William raised one eyebrow, questioning, and John saw there was nothing to be said. William was doing what had been asked of him; overmuch probing would hardly be fair. "No, it's all right," he said. "Thank you. I honor you, and I appreciate what you are doing. God bless you."

Indefinably, William's face softened. He bent his head in a respectful salute and left as quietly and unobtrusively as he had come.

☩　☩　☩

The sun shone bright and pouring hot on this July day with no wind as Abbot John crossed the court from the claustral buildings to the checker. He found a scene of quiet industry in the small stone building, its windows and doors open to let in any slight breeze. Brother Ambrose sat at one table spread with ledgers, perusing letters. William sat at another, behind piles of accounts, with a pen in his hand.

"How's it going?" John's tone was pleasantly friendly, the question apparently a general inquiry about the organizational affairs of the abbey.

"We are making good progress, thank you, Father John," beamed Brother Ambrose cheerfully. "It's always quite a busy time once we come fully into the shearing and the harvests: hiring and buying to be thought of, as well as selling. But we seem to be on top of all that's coming in and going out. Father William has cooled off from his initial whirlwind pace, for which I'm mighty grateful! I couldn't keep up with the speed of him at first; but ever since you had that trip away, he seems to have calmed down. He jogs along like any brother now. I think I've been a steadying influence on him."

The subject of this conversation did not reply but sat, the pen grasped loosely in his hand, his pale eyes watching their exchange without animation, his face betraying nothing as he listened.

Abbot John went to stand near him and looked over William's shoulder at the orderly sheets of accounts spread in front of him. On top of them lay a torn sheet of vellum, the ink of the words written on it still wet. It had been rejected from the scriptorium because too much erasing had worn a hole. Then it had been torn in two and torn in two again for other uses. On the small battered sheet that remained of the original, words newly scribed were quickly drying in the heat. John leaned over William's shoulder, silently reading it through twice . . . and again. William made no objection and sat quietly as John took the words in.

When we come plummeting down
Falling . . . falling . . .
When we lie hidden in the earth

Lost from sight
When we find the strength to lift up
When we ascend again toward the blue
When we rise up singing
And find our way to the sun
Then come tumbling down again
In freefall losing everything we gained
Our Lady of the Skylarks
Please pray for us.

"Yes. Some things cost more than we could ever have imagined," Abbot John said, his voice serious and sad, "but I think it will be worth it in the end."

Glossary of Terms

Ambra: measure of salt.

Breviary: monastic prayer book.

Ave Maria: prayer saluting Mary, the mother of Jesus, in quotation of Scripture, and beseeching her to pray for us.

Benedictine Rule: the document guiding daily life, written by St. Benedict.

Cellarer: monk responsible for oversight of all provisions; a key role in the community.

Chamber: a small, intimate room; sometimes specifically a bedroom.

Chapter: daily meeting governing practical matters, where a chapter of St. Benedict's Rule was read and expounded by the abbot.

Choir: the part of the church where the monastic community sits.

Cistercian: order of monks, a reform of Benedictine tradition.

Cloister: covered way giving access to main buildings of a monastery.

Cunning-folk: people with special wisdom or insight, possibly supernatural.

Dorter: dormitory.

Dwale: a mixture used in the Middle Ages as an anesthetic, containing hemlock, lettuce, bryony, henbane, opium, vinegar, and the bile of a pig.

Eucharist: Holy Communion meal, the Lord's Supper.

Externs: in an enclosed monastic order, nuns whose role was to provide the interface between the community and the world.

Frater: refectory.

Garth: garden quadrangle enclosed by the cloister.

Glebe land: land owned by the church.

Grail: chalice, the sacred cup holding the wine of the Eucharist.

Grand Silence: the longer period of complete abstention from speech beginning after Compline (the last office of the day) and lasting through the night until after Mass in the morning.

Hours: the services of worship in the monastic day.

Lay: not ordained.

Liturgy: structured worship.

Missal: book with the words for the Mass.

Nave: the body of the church occupied by the public in worship.

Obedience: the occupation allotted to a monk.

Obedientiary: monk with a particular office.

Office: the set worship taking place at regular intervals through the day.

Ostler, also hostler: man who looks after horses.

Palfrey: high-bred riding horse of the Middle Ages.

Pater Noster: the Lord's Prayer.

Physic: medicine.

Porter: doorkeeper.

Postern: a small door set within a large gate for ease of access.

Postulant: new member not yet made a novice.

Precentor: worship facilitator.

Prior: in an abbey, the deputy leader; in a priory, the leader.

Reredorter: latrines situated convenient to sleeping quarters.

Sacristan: monk with responsibility for the vestments and vessels, etc. of the altar.

"Salve Regina": hymn in honor of Mary, the mother of Jesus.

Skellig Michael: a steep rocky island near the Irish coast, inaccessible and bleak; this was the location of a very ascetic monastic order from the Dark Ages through to the Middle Ages.

Tarry wool: scraps of sheep's fleece snagged on thorns.

Villein: peasant legally tied to the land where he worked.

MONASTIC DAY

There may be slight variation from place to place and at different times from the Dark Ages through the Middle Ages and onward: for example, Vespers may be after supper rather than before. This gives a rough outline. Slight liberties are taken in my novels to allow human interactions to play out.

WINTER SCHEDULE (FROM MICHAELMAS)

2:30 a.m. Preparation for the nocturns of matins: psalms, etc.
3:00 a.m. Matins, with prayers for the royal family and for the dead.
5:00 a.m. Reading in preparation for Lauds.
6:00 a.m. Lauds at daybreak and Prime; wash and break fast (just bread and water, standing).
8.30 a.m. Terce, Morrow Mass, Chapter.
12:00 noon Sext, Sung Mass, midday meal.
2:00 p.m. None.
4:15 p.m. Vespers, Supper, Collatio.
6:15 p.m. Compline.
The Grand Silence begins

SUMMER SCHEDULE

1:30 a.m. Preparation for the nocturns of matins: psalms, etc.
2:00 a.m. Matins.
3:30 a.m. Lauds at daybreak, wash and break fast.
6:00 a.m. Prime, Morrow Mass, Chapter.
8:00 a.m. Terce, Sung Mass.
11:30 a.m. Sext, midday meal.
2:30 p.m. None.
5:30 p.m. Vespers, Supper, Collatio.
8:00 p.m. Compline.
The Grand Silence begins.

Liturgical Calendar

I have included the main feasts and fasts in the cycle of the church's year, plus one or two other dates that are mentioned (for example, Michaelmas and Lady Day when rents were traditionally collected) in these stories.

Advent: begins four Sundays before Christmas.
Christmas: December 25th.
Holy Innocents: December 28th.
Epiphany: January 6th.
Baptism of our Lord: concludes Christmastide, the Sunday after January 6th.
Candlemas: February 2 (Purification of Blessed Virgin Mary, Presentation of Christ in the temple).
Lent: Ash Wednesday to Holy Thursday; start date varies with phases of the moon.
Holy Week: last week of Lent and the Easter Triduum.
Easter Triduum (three days) of Good Friday, Holy Saturday, Easter Sunday.
Ascension: forty days after Easter.
Whitsun (Pentecost): fifty days after Easter.
Lady Day: May 31st.
Trinity Sunday: Sunday after Pentecost.
Corpus Christi: Thursday after Trinity Sunday.
Sacred Heart of Jesus: Friday of the following week.
Feast of John the Baptist: June 24th.
Lammas (literally "loaf-mass"; grain harvest): August 1st.
Michaelmas: feast of St. Michael and All Angels, September 29th.
All Saints: November 1st.
All Souls: November 2nd.
Martinmas: November 11th.

Also Available in
The Hawk and the Dove series

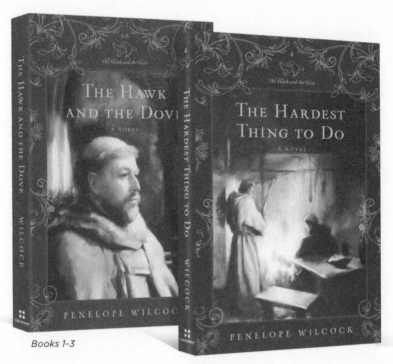

Books 1-3

Book 4

Coming July 2012!
REMEMBER ME
Book 6

Turn the page for an exciting preview of *Remember Me.*

Book 6 in *The Hawk and the Dove* series.

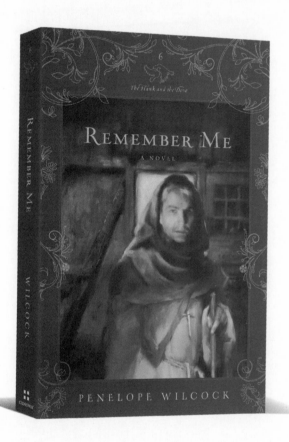

Coming in July 2012 to a bookstore near you.

CHAPTER
ONE

July

Like a subtle wraith of mist in the still-dark of the night in late
July he stole: silent and fleet, not hesitating. He came from the
northwest corner of the church, where a small door led out
into the abbey court from the side of the narthex. He did not
cross the court, but passed stealthily along the walk between
the yew-hedge and the perimeter wall. Swift and noiseless he
slipped along the close. It was a clear night but the dark of the
moon, and only the stars gave light at this hour of the morning. At the end of Lauds, as the brothers shuffled back up the
night stairs to resume their sleep, he had abstracted himself
so unobtrusively that no one had seen. He had dodged back
into the nave and stood in the deep shadows of the arcade in
the side aisle on the north side of the church, hardly breathing. When all was still, he opened the small door with utmost
caution; sliding the bolts back slowly and steadily without a
sound, drawing the door closed and lifting and dropping the
latch with barely a click, he left, and he was outside in the
freshness of the night. Such faint light as the stars gave out
found his silver hair, but that was the only glimmer of his presence as he slid from the abbey court along the close.

Peartree Cottage stood in the middle of the row of houses.
The wicket gate stood ajar, and he pushed it open without a
sound. As he stepped into the garden, the herbs gave up their

fragrance underfoot. He felt a slug fall into his sandal. He stooped to flick out the slug and to scratch up a handful of earth that he flung at the upstairs window. No response. He tried again. This time the casement was opened with irritable vigor from the inside, and Madeleine's voice said sharply, "Who is it?"

Peering down suspiciously into the garden she might not have seen him, but he moved very slightly and most quietly spoke her name.

"Whatever do *you* want?" she whispered then, surprised.

"Will you let me in?" She heard the soft-spoken words. And as she came in the dark down the narrow ladder stairway, she realized the implications of this visit. Naturally cautious, she asked herself, *Are you sure you welcome this?* Just in going down the stairs, in opening the door, she realized her heart was saying, *Yes.*

As quietly as she could, she drew back the bolts and turned the key, lifted the latch, and opened the door to him.

"Whatever has possessed you? What on earth do you think you're doing?" she whispered fiercely as he came into the room. "Shall I light the candle?"

"Nay, nay! There are no curtains, you might as well light a beacon," he said softly. "Can you not see?"

He himself had good night vision; it was an honest question.

"I wouldn't need to see!" she whispered back. "Who else would risk us both being thrown out by coming here at this time of the night? Are you certain no one saw you?"

"It's only a fool who is ever certain no one saw him. I surely hope not though, or we are done for, as you say."

In silence they stood then, not three feet between them in the warm darkness of the cottage. Embers tidied together on the hearth still glowed from the small fire Madeleine had lit to cook her supper. They gave out hardly any light at all: but between the embers and the stars, the shapes of things in the room and the man who stood before her could be clearly enough discerned.

"Well?" she said then. "What should I think? Why are you here?"

He stood silently. She waited for his reply. She knew well enough, but did not dare to presume what she hoped for.

"Do you . . ." His voice sounded unsure then; she heard the vulnerability in it. "Do you want me?"

Madeleine hesitated one last moment. There was still time to go back on this. She heard the intake of his breath in anxious uncertainty.

So she said in quick reassurance, "Of course I want you. With the whole of me. But is this honest? Isn't it stolen? Aren't we deceiving my brother?"

But he waited for no further discussion: she was in his embrace then, the ardent hold of yearning that she and he had waited for, it felt like so long. He did not kiss her, simply held her to him, his body pressed trembling against hers.

She closed her eyes and took in the feel of him; the heat of his hunger for her, the beating of his heart and his quickened breath—all of him, bone and muscle and skin, the soul of him that lit every part, the pulse of desire and destiny. She loved the touch of him, the smell of him. She knew by heart every mannerism, every trick of movement and expression, every inflection of his voice. In any crowd she would have turned at his footstep, knowing whom she heard.

"I had to come to you," he whispered, his face against her hair. "I couldn't think, I couldn't sleep; I haven't been able to concentrate on anything. I know I can't have you, I do know. But I need to have the memory of just one time together: for a refuge, for a viaticum—something real. I have been so desperate for you . . . to touch you . . . to hold you close to me . . . to feel your heartbeat and bury my face in your hair. Oh, my love, my love . . . I have *ached* to hold you."

She felt his hand lift to her head, caressing, and by the starlight she saw in his face such tenderness, such a flowing of love toward her as she had never imagined life might offer. He kissed her then, delicate kisses as light as a lacewing landing on a leaf: kissed her throat, her jaw, her cheekbones, her brow, kissed her eyelids closed, and then she felt his lips brush the curve of her cheek to find her mouth. He too closed his eyes as she parted her lips to the slow, beautiful, sensual rhapsody of his lover's kiss.

She felt the momentous tide of it overflow through all of her like the wave-swell of the sea; then before she could bear to let him go, he drew back from his kiss, but still holding her close. She wished she could see him properly, read the look in his eyes dark in the darkness.

"This is not what I thought," he whispered, "not what I expected."

He felt her body tense at his words and said hastily, "No! No, I didn't mean what you think. You are everything I want, all I long for! It's just that I had imagined this would lay things to rest; allow us to acknowledge something that is between us, and let it have its moment. I thought it might make it easier to relinquish it and give it back to God. But it doesn't feel like that now.

"Now that I am holding you I want never to have to let you go. I want us to share a bed and make love together, but I want us to share a home and make a life together too. I want time to discover all the things I don't know about you yet. I want to watch you washing at the sink in the morning as the sun comes streaming in through the open door. I want to watch you brushing your hair. I want to find you kneading dough for our loaf at the table when I come in with the firewood for our hearth. I want you to teach me about herbs and how to grow them."

"Brother Walafrid could teach you about that," she murmured.

"Yes, I know," he whispered, "but I don't feel the same about Brother Walafrid as I do about you."

She had rested her head against the hollow beneath his collar bone as she listened to these words. She heard the smile in his voice, and he bent his head to kiss the top of hers.

"When I entered monastic life," he said, in the quietest undertone, "it was for pragmatic reasons—I had no money, was the thing: and that's what keeps me there still; no money. I've heard men talk about vocation often enough, but I couldn't feel my way to it—didn't really know what they meant. I have never had a sense of vocation; until now.

"Now, all of me wants to be with all of you forever. Now I know what vocation is. But I am fifty years old, and I have no trade and no family. There is nothing I can offer you, and there is nowhere for us to go—even supposing you want me too.

"You asked me if this was honest. It's probably the most honest thing I've ever done in my life. I know it's beyond reach. If I come back here again, someone will see, it will be discovered somehow—these things always are; but I thought I could risk just this one time. And I can offer nothing more. You and I both, we depend on the charity of the community to house us; there are no other choices. Like the poor everywhere, we have no rights and no options. But one night, for pity's sake, just *one night!* And it's not even a night; only a miserly hour between the night office and Prime. But after this, you must not watch for me nor wait for me, for I shall not be able to come to you—not ever again; but, oh my darling, remember me, remember this hour we had. If you get a chance of happiness with someone else, take it with both hands, I shall not be jealous. And deceiving John? Up to a point. I won't tell him, and I won't let him see. But I wouldn't lie to him, and I won't pursue this. It's just that I couldn't have lived the rest of my life starving to hold you for *one time* close to me. Maybe it is stolen. Yes—it is. But a starving man will snatch a crust of bread, because it is life to him. And this is life to me."